Also by V. S. Naipaul

Fiction
THE MYSTIC MASSEUR
THE SUFFRAGE OF ELVIRA
MIGUEL STREET
A HOUSE FOR MR BISWAS
MR STONE AND THE KNIGHTS COMPANION
THE MIMIC MEN

Non-Fiction
THE MIDDLE PASSAGE
AN AREA OF DARKNESS

V. S. NAIPAUL

A Flag on the Island

THE MACMILLAN COMPANY, NEW YORK

COPYRIGHT © *1967* BY V. S. NAIPAUL

All rights reserved.
No part of this book may be reproduced
or transmitted in any form or by any means,
electronic or mechanical, including photocopying,
recording or by any information storage
and retrieval system, without permission in writing
from the Publisher.

Library of Congress Catalog Card Number: 68–19698

FIRST AMERICAN EDITION

First published in Great Britain in 1967
by Andre Deutsch Limited, London

The Macmillan Company, New York

Printed in the United States of America

TO DIANA ATHILL

All but two of the shorter pieces in this collection have appeared in periodicals in England or the United States. 'The Enemy' was written as part of my book *Miguel Street*. It was not used there, and some of the episodes were developed in later books; the present story was published in American *Vogue*. 'The Raffle' was written for the London *Evening Standard* series 'Did it Happen?' The answer was no; the autobiographical detail is deliberately misleading. *A Flag on the Island* was specially written for a film company. The story they required was to be 'musical' and comic and set in the Caribbean; it was to have a leading American character and many subsidiary characters; it was to have much sex and much dialogue; it was to be explicit.

Contents

My Aunt Gold Teeth

I never knew her real name and it is quite likely that she did have one, though I never heard her called anything but Gold Teeth. She did, indeed, have gold teeth. She had sixteen of them. She had married early and she had married well, and shortly after her marriage she exchanged her perfectly sound teeth for gold ones, to announce to the world that her husband was a man of substance.

Even without her gold teeth my aunt would have been noticeable. She was short, scarcely five foot, and she was very fat. If you saw her in silhouette you would have found it difficult to know whether she was facing you or whether she was looking sideways.

She ate little and prayed much. Her family being Hindu, and her husband being a pundit, she, too, was an orthodox Hindu. Of Hinduism she knew little apart from the ceremonies and the taboos, and this was enough for her. Gold Teeth saw God as a Power, and religious ritual as a means of harnessing that Power for great practical good, her good.

I may have given the impression that Gold Teeth prayed because she wanted to be less fat. The fact was that Gold Teeth had no children and she was almost forty. It was her childlessness, not her fat, that oppressed her, and she prayed for the curse to be removed. She was willing to try any means – any ritual, any prayer – in order to trap and channel the supernatural Power.

And so it was that she began to indulge in surreptitious Christian practices.

She was living at the time in a country village called

Cunupia, in County Caroni. Here the Canadian Mission had long waged war against the Indian heathen, and saved many. But Gold Teeth stood firm. The Minister of Cunupia expended his Presbyterian piety on her; so did the headmaster of the Mission school. But all in vain. At no time was Gold Teeth persuaded even to think about being converted. The idea horrified her. Her father had been in his day one of the best-known Hindu pundits, and even now her husband's fame as a pundit, as a man who could read and write Sanskrit, had spread far beyond Cunupia. She was in no doubt whatsoever that Hindus were the best people in the world, and that Hinduism was a superior religion. She was willing to select, modify and incorporate alien eccentricities into her worship; but to abjure her own faith – never!

Presbyterianism was not the only danger the good Hindu had to face in Cunupia. Besides, of course, the ever-present threat of open Muslim aggression, the Catholics were to be reckoned with. Their pamphlets were everywhere and it was hard to avoid them. In them Gold Teeth read of novenas and rosaries, of squads of saints and angels. These were things she understood and could even sympathize with, and they encouraged her to seek further. She read of the mysteries and the miracles, of penances and indulgences. Her scepticism sagged, and yielded to a quickening, if reluctant, enthusiasm.

One morning she took the train for the County town of Chaguanas, three miles, two stations and twenty minutes away. The Church of St Philip and St James in Chaguanas stands imposingly at the end of the Caroni Savannah Road, and although Gold Teeth knew Chaguanas well, all she knew of the church was that it had a clock, at which she had glanced on her way to the railway station nearby. She had hitherto been far more interested in the drab ochre-washed edifice opposite, which was the police station.

She carried herself into the churchyard, awed by her own temerity, feeling like an explorer in a land of cannibals. To her relief, the church was empty. It was not as terrifying as she had expected. In the gilt and images and the resplendent cloths she found much that reminded her of her Hindu temple. Her eyes caught a discreet sign: CANDLES TWO CENTS EACH. She undid the knot in the end of her veil, where she kept her money, took out three cents, popped them into the box, picked up a candle and muttered a prayer in Hindustani. A brief moment of elation gave way to a sense of guilt, and she was suddenly anxious to get away from the church as fast as her weight would let her.

She took a bus home, and hid the candle in her chest of drawers. She had half feared that her husband's Brahminical flair for clairvoyance would have uncovered the reason for her trip to Chaguanas. When after four days, which she spent in an ecstasy of prayer, her husband had mentioned nothing, Gold Teeth thought it safe to burn the candle. She burned it secretly at night, before her Hindu images, and sent up, as she thought, prayers of double efficacy.

Every day her religious schizophrenia grew, and presently she began wearing a crucifix. Neither her husband nor her neighbours knew she did so. The chain was lost in the billows of fat around her neck, and the crucifix was itself buried in the valley of her gargantuan breasts. Later she acquired two holy pictures, one of the Virgin Mary, the other of the crucifixion, and took care to conceal them from her husband. The prayers she offered to these Christian things filled her with new hope and buoyancy. She became an addict of Christianity.

Then her husband, Ramprasad, fell ill.

Ramprasad's sudden, unaccountable illness alarmed Gold Teeth. It was, she knew, no ordinary illness, and she knew, too, that her religious transgression was the cause. The District Medical Officer at Chaguanas said it was diabetes, but Gold Teeth knew better. To be on the safe side, though, she used the insulin he prescribed and, to be even safer, she consulted Ganesh Pundit, the masseur with mystic leanings, celebrated as a faith-healer.

Ganesh came all the way from Fuente Grove to Cunupia. He came in great humility, anxious to serve Gold Teeth's husband, for Gold Teeth's husband was a Brahmin among

Brahmins, a *Panday*, a man who knew all five Vedas; while he, Ganesh, was a mere *Chaubay* and knew only four.

With spotless white *koortah*, his dhoti cannily tied, and a tasselled green scarf as a concession to elegance, Ganesh exuded the confidence of the professional mystic. He looked at the sick man, observed his pallor, sniffed the air. 'This man,' he said, 'is bewitched. Seven spirits are upon him.'

He was telling Gold Teeth nothing she didn't know. She had known from the first that there were spirits in the affair, but she was glad that Ganesh had ascertained their number.

'But you mustn't worry,' Ganesh added. 'We will "tie" the house – in spiritual bonds – and no spirit will be able to come in.'

Then, without being asked, Gold Teeth brought out a blanket, folded it, placed it on the floor and invited Ganesh to sit on it. Next she brought him a brass jar of fresh water, a mango leaf and a plate full of burning charcoal.

'Bring me some ghee,' Ganesh said, and after Gold Teeth had done so, he set to work. Muttering continuously in Hindustani he sprinkled the water from the brass jar around him with the mango leaf. Then he melted the ghee in the fire and the charcoal hissed so sharply that Gold Teeth could not make out his words. Presently he rose and said, 'You must put some of the ash of this fire on your husband's forehead, but if he doesn't want you to do that, mix it with his food. You must keep the water in this jar and place it every night before your front door.'

Gold Teeth pulled her veil over her forehead.

Ganesh coughed. 'That,' he said, rearranging his scarf, 'is all. There is nothing more I can do. God will do the rest.'

He refused payment for his services. It was enough honour, he said, for a man as humble as he was to serve Pundit Ramprasad, and she, Gold Teeth, had been singled out by fate to be the spouse of such a worthy man. Gold Teeth received the impression that Ganesh spoke from a first-hand knowledge of fate and its designs, and her heart, buried deep down under inches of mortal, flabby flesh, sank a little.

'Baba,' she said hesitantly, 'revered Father, I have something to say to you.' But she couldn't say anything more and Ganesh, seeing this, filled his eyes with charity and love.

'What is it, my child?'

'I have done a great wrong, Baba.'

'What sort of wrong?' he asked, and his tone indicated that Gold Teeth could do no wrong.

'I have prayed to Christian things.'

And to Gold Teeth's surprise, Ganesh chuckled benevolently. 'And do you think God minds, daughter? There is only one God and different people pray to Him in different ways. It doesn't matter how you pray, but God is pleased if you pray at all.'

'So it is not because of me that my husband has fallen ill?'

'No, to be sure, daughter.'

In his professional capacity Ganesh was consulted by people of many faiths, and with the licence of the mystic he had exploited the commodiousness of Hinduism, and made room for all beliefs. In this way he had many clients, as he called them, many satisfied clients.

Henceforward Gold Teeth not only pasted Ramprasad's pale forehead with the sacred ash Ganesh had prescribed, but mixed substantial amounts with his food. Ramprasad's appetite, enormous even in sickness, diminished; and he shortly entered into a visible and alarming decline that mystified his wife.

She fed him more ash than before, and when it was exhausted and Ramprasad perilously macerated, she fell back on the Hindu wife's last resort. She took her husband home to her mother. That venerable lady, my grandmother, lived with us in Port-of-Spain.

Ramprasad was tall and skeletal, and his face was grey. The virile voice that had expounded a thousand theological points and recited a hundred *puranas* was now a wavering whisper. We cooped him up in a room called, oddly, 'the pantry'. It had never been used as a pantry and one can only assume that the architect had so designated it some forty

years before. It was a tiny room. If you wished to enter the
pantry you were compelled, as soon as you opened the door,
to climb on to the bed: it fitted the room to a miracle. The
lower half of the walls were concrete, the upper close lattice-
work; there were no windows.

My grandmother had her doubts about the suitability of
the room for a sick man. She was worried about the lattice-
work. It let in air and light, and Ramprasad was not going to
die from these things if she could help it. With cardboard,
oil-cloth and canvas she made the lattice-work air-proof and
light-proof.

And, sure enough, within a week Ramprasad's appetite
returned, insatiable and insistent as before. My grandmother
claimed all the credit for this, though Gold Teeth knew that
the ash she had fed him had not been without effect. Then she
realized with horror that she had ignored a very important
thing. The house in Cunupia had been tied and no spirits
could enter, but the house in the city had been given
no such protection and any spirit could come and go as it
chose. The problem was pressing.

Ganesh was out of the question. By giving his services
free he had made it impossible for Gold Teeth to call him in
again. But thinking in this way of Ganesh, she remembered
his words: 'It doesn't matter how you pray, but God is
pleased if you pray at all.'

Why not, then, bring Christianity into play again?

She didn't want to take any chances this time. She decided
to tell Ramprasad.

He was propped up in bed, and eating. When Gold Teeth
opened the door he stopped eating and blinked at the un-
wonted light. Gold Teeth, stepping into the doorway and
filling it, shadowed the room once more and he went on
eating. She placed the palms of her hands on the bed. It
creaked.

'Man,' she said.

Ramprasad continued to eat.

'Man,' she said in English, 'I thinking about going to the

church to pray. You never know, and it better to be on the safe side. After all, the house ain't tied – '

'I don't want you to pray in no church,' he whispered, in English too.

Gold Teeth did the only thing she could do. She began to cry.

Three days in succession she asked his permission to go to church, and his opposition weakened in the face of her tears. He was now, besides, too weak to oppose anything. Although his appetite had returned, he was still very ill and very weak, and every day his condition became worse.

On the fourth day he said to Gold Teeth, 'Well, pray to Jesus and go to church, if it will put your mind at rest.'

And Gold Teeth straight away set about putting her mind at rest. Every morning she took the trolley-bus to the Holy Rosary Church, to offer worship in her private way. Then she was emboldened to bring a crucifix and pictures of the Virgin and the Messiah into the house. We were all somewhat worried by this, but Gold Teeth's religious nature was well known to us; her husband was a learned pundit and when all was said and done this was an emergency, a matter of life and death. So we could do nothing but look on. Incense and camphor and ghee burned now before the likeness of Krishna and Shiva as well as Mary and Jesus. Gold Teeth revealed an appetite for prayer that equalled her husband's for food, and we marvelled at both, if only because neither prayer nor food seemed to be of any use to Ramprasad.

One evening, shortly after bell and gong and conch-shell had announced that Gold Teeth's official devotions were almost over, a sudden chorus of lamentation burst over the house, and I was summoned to the room reserved for prayer. 'Come quickly, something dreadful has happened to your aunt.'

The prayer-room, still heavy with fumes of incense, presented an extraordinary sight. Before the Hindu shrine, flat on her face, Gold Teeth lay prostrate, rigid as a sack of flour. I had only seen Gold Teeth standing or sitting, and the aspect of Gold Teeth prostrate, so novel and so grotesque, was disturbing.

My grandmother, an alarmist by nature, bent down and put her ear to the upper half of the body on the floor. 'I don't seem to hear her heart,' she said.

We were all somewhat terrified. We tried to lift Gold Teeth but she seemed as heavy as lead. Then, slowly, the body quivered. The flesh beneath the clothes rippled, then billowed, and the children in the room sharpened their shrieks. Instinctively we all stood back from the body and waited to see what was going to happen. Gold Teeth's hand began to pound the floor and at the same time she began to gurgle.

My grandmother had grasped the situation. 'She's got the spirit,' she said.

At the word 'spirit', the children shrieked louder, and my grandmother slapped them into silence.

The gurgling resolved itself into words pronounced with a lingering ghastly quaver. 'Hail Mary, Hare Ram,' Gold Teeth said, 'the snakes are after me. Everywhere snakes. Seven snakes. Rama! Rama! Full of grace. Seven spirits leaving Cunupia by the four-o'clock train for Port-of-Spain.'

My grandmother and my mother listened eagerly, their faces lit up with pride. I was rather ashamed at the exhibition, and annoyed with Gold Teeth for putting me into a fright. I moved towards the door.

'Who is that going away? Who is the young *caffar*, the unbeliever?' the voice asked abruptly.

'Come back quickly, boy,' my grandmother whispered. 'Come back and ask her pardon.'

I did as I was told.

'It is all right, son,' Gold Teeth replied, 'you don't know. You are young.'

Then the spirit appeared to leave her. She wrenched herself up to a sitting position and wondered why we were all there. For the rest of that evening she behaved as if nothing had happened, and she pretended she didn't notice that everyone was looking at her and treating her with unusual respect.

'I have always said it, and I will say it again,' my grandmother said, 'that these Christians are very religious people. That is why I encouraged Gold Teeth to pray to Christian things.'

Ramprasad died early next morning and we had the announcement on the radio after the local news at one o'clock. Ramprasad's death was the only one announced and so, although it came between commercials, it made some impression. We buried him that afternoon in Mucurapo Cemetery.

As soon as we got back my grandmother said, 'I have always said it, and I will say it again: I don't like these Christian things. Ramprasad would have got better if only you, Gold Teeth, had listened to me and not gone running after these Christian things.'

Gold Teeth sobbed her assent; and her body squabbered and shook as she confessed the whole story of her trafficking with Christianity. We listened in astonishment and shame. We didn't know that a good Hindu, and a member of our family, could sink so low. Gold Teeth beat her breast and pulled ineffectually at her long hair and begged to be forgiven. 'It is all my fault,' she cried. 'My own fault, Ma. I fell in a moment of weakness. Then I just couldn't stop.'

My grandmother's shame turned to pity. 'It's all right, Gold Teeth. Perhaps it was this you needed to bring you back to your senses.'

That evening Gold Teeth ritually destroyed every reminder of Christianity in the house.

'You have only yourself to blame,' my grandmother said, 'if you have no children now to look after you.'

1954

The Raffle

They don't pay primary school teachers a lot in Trinidad, but they allow them to beat their pupils as much as they want.

Mr Hinds, my teacher, was a big beater. On the shelf below *The Last of England* he kept four or five tamarind rods. They are good for beating. They are limber, they sting and they last. There was a tamarind tree in the schoolyard. In his locker Mr Hinds also kept a leather strap soaking in the bucket of water every class had in case of fire.

It wouldn't have been so bad if Mr Hinds hadn't been so young and athletic. At the one school sports I went to, I saw him slip off his shining shoes, roll up his trousers neatly to mid-shin and win the Teachers' Hundred Yards, a cigarette between his lips, his tie flapping smartly over his shoulder. It was a wine-coloured tie: Mr Hinds was careful about his dress. That was something else that somehow added to the terror. He wore a brown suit, a cream shirt and the wine-coloured tie.

It was also rumoured that he drank heavily at week-ends.

But Mr Hinds had a weak spot. He was poor. We knew he gave those 'private lessons' because he needed the extra money. He gave us private lessons in the ten-minute morning recess. Every boy paid fifty cents for that. If a boy didn't pay, he was kept in all the same and flogged until he paid.

We also knew that Mr Hinds had an allotment in Morvant where he kept some poultry and a few animals.

The other boys sympathized with us – needlessly. Mr Hinds beat us, but I believe we were all a little proud of him.

I say he beat us, but I don't really mean that. For some reason which I could never understand then and can't now, Mr Hinds never beat me. He never made me clean the blackboard. He never made me shine his shoes with the duster. He even called me by my first name, Vidiadhar.

This didn't do me any good with the other boys. At cricket I wasn't allowed to bowl or keep wicket and I always went in at number eleven. My consolation was that I was spending only two terms at the school before going on to Queen's Royal College. I didn't want to go to QRC so much as I wanted to get away from Endeavour (that was the name of the school). Mr Hinds's favour made me feel insecure.

At private lessons one morning Mr Hinds announced that he was going to raffle a goat – a shilling a chance.

He spoke with a straight face and nobody laughed. He made me write out the names of all the boys in the class on two foolscap sheets. Boys who wanted to risk a shilling had to put a tick after their names. Before private lessons ended there was a tick after every name.

I became very unpopular. Some boys didn't believe there was a goat. They all said that if there was a goat, they knew who was going to get it. I hoped they were right. I had long wanted an animal of my own, and the idea of getting milk from my own goat attracted me. I had heard that Mannie Ramjohn, Trinidad's champion miler, trained on goat's milk and nuts.

Next morning I wrote out the names of the boys on slips of paper. Mr Hinds borrowed my cap, put the slips in, took one out, said, 'Vidiadhar, is your goat,' and immediately threw all the slips into the wastepaper basket.

At lunch I told my mother, 'I win a goat today.'

'What sort of goat?'

'I don't know. I ain't see it.'

She laughed. She didn't believe in the goat, either. But when she finished laughing she said: 'It would be nice, though.'

I was getting not to believe in the goat, too. I was afraid to ask Mr Hinds, but a day or two later he said, 'Vidiadhar, you coming or you ain't coming to get your goat?'

He lived in a tumbledown wooden house in Woodbrook and when I got there I saw him in khaki shorts, vest and blue canvas shoes. He was cleaning his bicycle with a yellow flannel. I was overwhelmed. I had never associated him with such dress and such a menial labour. But his manner was more ironic and dismissing than in the classroom.

He led me to the back of the yard. There *was* a goat. A white one with big horns, tied to a plum tree. The ground around the tree was filthy. The goat looked sullen and sleepy-eyed, as if a little stunned by the smell it had made. Mr Hinds invited me to stroke the goat. I stroked it. He closed his eyes and went on chewing. When I stopped stroking him, he opened his eyes.

Every afternoon at about five an old man drove a donkey-cart through Miguel Street where we lived. The cart was piled with fresh grass tied into neat little bundles, so neat you felt grass wasn't a thing that grew but was made in a factory somewhere. That donkey-cart became important to my mother and me. We were buying five, sometimes six bundles a day, and every bundle cost six cents. The goat didn't change. He still looked sullen and bored. From time to time Mr Hinds asked me with a smile how the goat was getting on, and I said it was getting on fine. But when I asked my mother when we were going to get milk from the goat, she told me to stop aggravating her. Then one day she put up a sign:

RAM FOR SERVICE
Apply Within For Terms

and got very angry when I asked her to explain it.

The sign made no difference. We bought the neat bundles of grass, the goat ate, and I saw no milk.

And when I got home one lunch-time I saw no goat.

'Somebody borrow it,' my mother said. She looked happy.

'When it coming back?'

She shrugged her shoulders.

It came back that afternoon. When I turned the corner into Miguel Street I saw it on the pavement outside our house. A man I didn't know was holding it by a rope and making a big row, gesticulating like anything with his free hand. I knew that sort of man. He wasn't going to let hold of the rope until he had said his piece. A lot of people were looking on through curtains.

'But why all-you want to rob poor people so?' he said, shouting. He turned to his audience behind the curtains. 'Look, all-you, just look at this goat!'

The goat, limitlessly impassive, chewed slowly, its eyes half-closed.

'But how all you people so advantageous? My brother stupid and he ain't know this goat, but I know this goat. Everybody in Trinidad who know about goat know this goat, from Icacos to Mayaro to Toco to Chaguaramas,' he said, naming the four corners of Trinidad. 'Is the most uselessest goat in the whole world. And you charge my brother for this goat? Look, you better give me back my brother money, you hear.'

My mother looked hurt and upset. She went inside and came out with some dollar notes. The man took them and handed over the goat.

That evening my mother said, 'Go and tell your Mr Hinds that I don't want this goat here.'

Mr Hinds didn't look surprised. 'Don't want it, eh?' He thought, and passed a well-trimmed thumb-nail over his moustache. 'Look, tell you. Going to buy him back. Five dollars.'

I said, 'He eat more than that in grass alone.'

That didn't surprise him either. 'Say six, then.'

I sold. That, I thought, was the end of that.

One Monday afternoon about a month before the end of my last term I announced to my mother, 'That goat raffling again.'

She became alarmed.

At tea on Friday I said casually, 'I win the goat.'

She was expecting it. Before the sun set a man had brought the goat away from Mr Hinds, given my mother some money and taken the goat away.

I hoped Mr Hinds would never ask about the goat. He did, though. Not the next week, but the week after that, just before school broke up.

I didn't know what to say.

But a boy called Knolly, a fast bowler and a favourite victim of Mr Hinds, answered for me. 'What goat?' he whispered loudly. 'That goat kill and eat long time.'

Mr Hinds was suddenly furious. 'Is true, Vidiadhar?'

I didn't nod or say anything. The bell rang and saved me.

At lunch I told my mother, 'I don't want to go back to that school.'

She said, 'You must be brave.'

I didn't like the argument, but I went.

We had Geography the first period.

'Naipaul,' Mr Hinds said right away, forgetting my first name, 'define a peninsula.'

'Peninsula,' I said, 'a piece of land entirely surrounded by water.'

'Good. Come up here.' He went to the locker and took out the soaking leather strap. Then he fell on me. 'You sell my goat?' Cut. 'You kill my goat?' Cut. 'How you so damn ungrateful?' Cut, cut, cut. 'Is the last time you win anything I raffle.'

It was the last day I went to that school.

1957

A Christmas Story

Though it is Christmas Eve my mind is not on Christmas. I look forward instead to the day after Boxing Day, for on that day the inspectors from the Audit Department in Port-of-Spain will be coming down to the village where the new school has been built. I await their coming with calm. There is still time, of course, to do all that is necessary. But I shall not do it, though my family, from whom the spirit of Christmas has, alas, also fled, have been begging me to lay aside my scruples, my new-found faith, and to rescue us all from disgrace and ruin. It is in my power to do so, but there comes a time in every man's life when he has to take a stand. This time, I must confess, has come very late for me.

It seems that everything has come late to me. I continued a Hindu, though of that religion I saw and knew little save meaningless and shameful rites, until I was nearly eighteen. Why I so continued I cannot explain. Perhaps it was the inertia with which that religion deadens its devotees. It did not, after all, require much intelligence to see that Hinduism, with its animistic rites, its idolatry, its emphasis on mango leaf, banana leaf and – the truth is the truth – cowdung, was a religion little fitted for the modern world. I had only to contrast the position of the Hindus with that of the Christians. I had only to consider the differing standards of dress, houses, food. Such differences have today more or less disappeared, and the younger generation will scarcely understand what I mean. I might even be reproached with laying too great a stress on the superficial. What can I say? Will I be believed if I say that to me the superficial has always symbolized the profound? But it is enough, I feel, to state that at eighteen my eyes were opened. I did not have to be 'converted' by the Presbyterians of the Canadian Mission. I had only to look at the work they were doing among the backward Hindus and Moslems of my district. I had only to look at their schools, to look at the houses of the converted.

My Presbyterianism, then, though late in coming, affected me deeply. I was interested in teaching – there was no other thing a man of my limited means and limited education could do – and my Presbyterianism was a distinct advantage. It gave me a grace in the eyes of my superiors. It also enabled me to be a good teacher, for between what I taught and what I felt there was no discordance. How different the position of those who, still unconverted, attempted to teach in Presbyterian schools!

And now that the time for frankness has come, I must also remark on the pleasure my new religion gave me. It was a pleasure to hear myself called Randolph, a name of rich historical associations, a name, I feel, thoroughly attuned to the times in which we live and to the society in which I found myself, and to forget that once – I still remember it with shame – I answered, with simple instinct, to the name of – Choonilal. That, however, is so much in the past. I have buried it. Yet I remember it now, not only because the time for frankness has come, but because only two weeks ago my son Winston, going through some family papers – clearly the boy had no right to be going through my private papers, but he shares his mother's curiosity – came upon the name. He teased, indeed reproached me, with it, and in a fit of anger, for which I am now grievously sorry and for which I must make time, while time there still is, to apologize to him, in a fit of anger I gave him a sound thrashing, such as I often gave in my school-teaching days to those pupils whose persistent shortcomings were matched by the stupidity and backwardness of their parents. Backwardness has always roused me to anger.

As much as by the name Randolph, pleasure was given me
by the stately and *clean* – there is no other word for it –
rituals sanctioned by my new religion. How agreeable, for
instance, to rise early on a Sunday morning, to bathe and
breakfast and then, in the most spotless of garments, to walk
along the still quiet and cool roads to our place of worship,
and there to see the most respectable and respected, all
dressed with a similar purity, addressing themselves to the
devotions in which I myself could participate, after for long
being an outsider, someone to whom the words *Christ* and
Father meant no more than *winter* or *autumn* or *daffodil*. Such
of the unconverted village folk who were energetic enough to
be awake and alert at that hour gaped at us as we walked in
white procession to our church. And though their admiration
was sweet, I must confess that at the same time it filled me
with shame to reflect that not long before I too formed part
of the gaping crowd. To walk past their gaze was peculiarly
painful to me, for I, more perhaps than anyone in that slow
and stately procession, *knew* – and by my silence had for
nearly eighteen years condoned – the practices those people
indulged in in the name of religion. My attitude towards them
was therefore somewhat stern, and it gave me some little
consolation to know that though we were in some ways
alike, we were distinguished from them not only by our
names, which after all no man carries pinned to his lapel,
but also by our dress. On these Sundays of which I speak the
men wore trousers and jackets of white drill, quite unlike the
leg-revealing dhoti which it still pleased those others to wear,
a garment which I have always felt makes the wearer ridiculous. I even sported a white solar topee. The girls and ladies
wore the short frocks which the others held in abhorrence;
they wore hats; in every respect, I am pleased to say, they
resembled their sisters who had come all the way from
Canada and other countries to work among our people. I
might be accused of laying too much stress on superficial
things. But I ought to say in my own defence that it is my
deeply held conviction that progress is not a matter of

outward show, but an attitude of mind; and it was this that my religion gave me.

It might seem from what I have so far said that the embracing of Presbyterianism conferred only benefits and pleasure. I wish to make no great fuss of the trials I had to endure, but it is sufficient to state that, while at school and in other associations my fervent adherence to my new faith was viewed with favour, I had elsewhere to put up with the constant ridicule of those of my relations who continued, in spite of my example, in the ways of darkness. They spoke my name, Randolph, with accents of the purest mockery. I bore this with fortitude. It was what I expected, and I was greatly strengthened by my faith, as a miser is by the thought of his gold. In time, when they saw that their ridiculing of my name had not the slightest effect on me – on the contrary, whereas before I had in my signature suppressed my first name behind the blank initial C, now I spelt out Randolph in full – in time they desisted.

But that was not the end of my trials. I had up to that time eaten with my fingers, a manner of eating which is now so repulsive to me, so ugly, so unhygienic, that I wonder how I managed to do it until my eighteenth year. Yet I must now confess that at that time food never tasted as sweet as when eaten with the fingers, and that my first attempts to eat with the proper implements of knife and fork and spoon were almost in the nature of shameful experiments, furtively carried out; and even when I was by myself I could not get rid of the feeling of self-consciousness. It was easier to get used to the name of Randolph than to knife and fork.

Eating, then, in my determined manner one Sunday lunchtime, I heard that I had a visitor. It was a man; he didn't knock, but came straight into my room, and I knew at once that he was a relation. These people have never learned to knock or to close doors behind them.

I must confess I felt somewhat foolish to be caught with those implements in my hand.

'Hello, Randolph,' the boy Hori said, pronouncing the name in a most offensive manner.

'Good afternoon, *Hori*.'

He remained impervious to my irony. This boy, Hori, was the greatest of my tormentors. He was also the grossest. He strained charity. He was a great lump of a man and he gloried in his brutishness. He fancied himself a debater as well, and many were the discussions and arguments we had had, this lout – he strained charity, as I have said – insisting that to squat on the ground and eat off banana leaves was hygienic and proper, that knives and forks were dirty because used again and again by various persons, whereas the fingers were personal and could always be made thoroughly clean by washing. But he never had *his* fingers clean, that I knew.

'Eating, Randolph?'

'I am having my lunch, *Hori*.'

'Beef, Randolph. You are progressing, Randolph.'

'I am glad you note it, *Hori*.'

I cannot understand why these people should persist in this admiration for the cow, which has always seemed to me a filthy animal, far filthier than the pig, which they abhor. Yet it must be stated that this eating of beef was the most strenuous of my tests. If I persevered it was only because I was strengthened by my faith. But to be found at this juncture – I was in my Sunday suit of white drill, my prayer book was on the table, my white solar topee on the wall, and I was eating beef with knife and fork – to be found thus by Hori was a trifle embarrassing. I must have looked the picture of the over-zealous convert.

My instinct was to ask him to leave. But it occurred to me that that would have been too easy, too cowardly a way out. Instead, I plied my knife and fork with as much skill as I could command at that time. He sat, not on a chair, but on the table, just next to my plate, the lout, and gazed at me while I ate. Ignoring his smile, I ate, as one might eat of sacrificial food. He crossed his fat legs, leaned back on his palms and examined me. I paid no attention. Then he took one of the forks that were about and began picking his teeth with it. I was angry and revolted. Tears sprang to my eyes. I rose, pushed away my plate, pushed back my chair, and asked him to leave. The violence of my reaction surprised him, and he did as I asked. As soon as he had gone I took the fork he had handled and bent it and stamped on it and then threw it out of the window.

Progress, as I have said, is an attitude of mind. And if I relate this trifling incident with such feeling, it is because it demonstrates how difficult that attitude of mind is to acquire, for there are hundreds who are ready to despise and ridicule those who they think are getting above themselves. And let people say what they will, the contempt even of the foolish is hard to bear. Let no one think, therefore, that my new religion did not bring its share of trials and tribulations. But I was sufficiently strengthened by my faith to bear them all with fortitude.

My life thereafter was a lonely one. I had cut myself off from my family, and from those large family gatherings which had hitherto given me so much pleasure and comfort, for always, I must own, at the back of my mind there had been the thought that in the event of real trouble there would be people to whom I could turn. Now I was deprived of this solace. I stuck to my vocation with a dedication which surprised even myself. To be a teacher it is necessary to be taught; and after much difficulty I managed to have myself sent to the Training College in Port-of-Spain. The competition for these places was fierce, and for many years I was passed over, because there were many others who were more fitting. Some indeed had been born of Presbyterian parents. But my zeal, which ever mounted as the failures multiplied, eventually was rewarded. I was twenty-eight when I was sent to the Training College, considerably older than most of the trainees.

It was no pleasure to me to note that during those ten years the boy Hori had been prospering. He had gone into the trucking business and he had done remarkably well. He had bought a second truck, then a third, and it seemed that to his success there could be no limit, while my own was always restricted to the predictable contents of the brown-paper pay-packet at the end of the month. The clothes in which I had taken such pride at first became less resplendent, until I felt it as a disgrace to go to church in them. But it became clear to me that this was yet another of the trials I was called upon to undergo, and I endured it, until I almost took pleasure in the darns on my sleeves and elbows.

At this time I was invited to the wedding of Hori's son, Kedar. They marry young, these people! It was an occasion which surmounted religious differences, and it was a distinct pleasure to me to be again with the family, for their attitude had changed. They had become reconciled to my Presbyterianism and indeed treated me with respect for my profession, a respect which, I fear, was sometimes missing in the attitude of my superiors and even my pupils. The marriage rites distressed me. The make-shift though beautiful tent, the coconut-palm arches hung with clusters of fruit, the use of things like mango leaves and grass and saffron, the sacrificial fire, all these things filled me with shame rather than delight. But the rites were only a small part of the celebrations. There was much good food, strictly vegetarian but somehow extremely tempting; and after a period of distaste for Indian food, I had come back to it again. The food, I say, was rich. The music and the dances were thrilling. The tent and the illuminations had a charm which not even our school hall had on concert nights, though the marriage ceremony did not of course have the grace and dignity of those conducted, as proper marriages should be, in a church.

Kedar received a fabulous dowry, and his bride, of whose face I had just a glimpse when her silk veil was parted, was indeed beautiful. But such beauty has always appeared to me skin deep. Beauty in women is a disturbing thing. But beyond the beauty it is always necessary to look for the greater qualities of manners and – a thing I always remind Winston of – no one is too young or too old to learn – manners and *ways*. She was beautiful. It was sad to think of her joined to Kedar for life, but she was perhaps fitted for nothing else. No need to speak of the resplendent regalia of Kedar himself: his turban, the crown with tassels and pendant glass, his richly embroidered silk jacket, and all those othe adornments which for that night concealed so well the truck-driver that he was.

I left the wedding profoundly saddened. I could not help reflecting on my own position and contrasting it with Hori's or even Kedar's. I was now over forty, and marriage, which in the normal way would have come to me at the age of twenty or thereabouts, was still far from me. This was my own fault. Arranged marriages like Kedar's had no part in my scheme of things. I wished to marry, as the person says in *The Vicar of Wakefield*, someone who had qualities that would wear well. My choice was severely restricted. I wished to marry a Presbyterian lady who was intelligent, well brought up and educated, and wished to marry me. This last condition, alas, I could find few willing to fulfil. And indeed I had little to offer. Among Hindus it would have been otherwise. There might have been men of substance who would have been willing to marry their daughters to a teacher, to acquire respectability and the glamour of a learned profession. Such a position has its strains, of course, for it means that the daughter remains, as it were, subject to her family; but the position is not without its charms.

You might imagine – and you would be correct – that at this time my faith was undergoing its severest strain. How often I was on the point of reneging I shudder to tell. I felt myself about to yield; I stiffened in my devotions and prayers. I reflected on the worthlessness of worldly things, but this was a reflection I found few to share. I might add here, in parenthesis and without vanity, that I had had several offers from the fathers of unconverted daughters, whose only condition was the one, about my religion, which I could not accept; for my previous caste had made me acceptable to many.

In this situation of doubt, of nightly wrestling with God, an expression whose meaning I came only then fully to understand, my fortune changed. I was appointed a headmaster. Now I can speak! How many people know of the tribulations, the pettiness, the intrigue which schoolteachers have to undergo to obtain such promotion? Such jockeying, such jealousy, such ill-will comes into play. What can I say of the advances one has to make, the rebuffs one has to suffer in silence, the waiting, the undoing of the unworthy who seek to push themselves forward for positions which they are ill-qualified to fill but which, by glibness and all the outward shows of respectability and efficiency and piety, they manage to persuade our superiors that they alone can fill? I too had my adversaries. My chief rival – but let him rest in peace! I am, I trust, a Christian, and will do no man the injustice of imagining him to persist in error even after we have left this vale of tears.

In my fortune, so opportune, I saw the hand of God. I speak in all earnestness. For without this I would surely have lapsed into the ways of darkness, for who among us can so steel himself as to resist temptation for all time? In my gratitude I applied myself with renewed dedication to my task. And it was this that doubtless evoked the gratification of my superiors which was to lead to my later elevation. For at a time when most men, worn out by the struggle, are content to relax, I showed myself more eager than before. I instituted prayers four times a day. I insisted on attendance at Sunday School. I taught Sunday School myself, and with the weight of my influence persuaded the other teachers to do likewise, so that Sunday became another day for us, a day of rest which we consumed with work for the Lord.

And I did not neglect the educational side. The blackboards all now sparkled with diagrams in chalks of various colours, projects which we had in hand. Oh, the school was such a pretty sight then! I instituted a rigid system of discipline, and forbade indiscriminate flogging by pupil teachers. All flogging I did myself on Friday afternoons, sitting in impartial judgment, as it were, on the school, on pupils as well as teachers. It is surely a better system, and I am glad to say that it has now been adopted throughout the island. The most apt pupils I kept after school, and for some trifling extra fee gave them private lessons. And the school became so involved with work as an ideal that had to be joyously pursued and not as something that had to be endured, that the usefulness of these private lessons was widely appreciated, and soon larger numbers than I could cope with were staying after school for what they affectionately termed their 'private'.

And I married. It was now in my power to marry virtually anyone I pleased, and there were among the Sunday School staff not a few who made their attachment to me plain. I am not such a bad-looking fellow! But I wished to marry someone who had qualities that would wear well. I was nearly fifty. I did not wish to marry someone who was much younger than myself. And it was my good fortune at this juncture to receive an offer – I hesitate to use this word, which sounds so much like the Hindu custom and reminds one of the real estate business, but here I must be frank – from no less a person than a schools inspector, who had an unmarried daughter of thirty-five, a woman neglected by the men of the island because of her attainments – yes, you read right – which were considerable, but not of the sort that proclaims itself to the world. In our attitude to women much remains to be changed! I have often, during these past days, reflected on marriage. Such a turning, a point in time whence so many consequences flow. I wonder what Winston, poor boy, will do when his time comes.

My establishment could not rival Hori's or Kedar's for splendour, but within it there was peace and culture such as I had long dreamed of. It was a plain wooden house, but well built, built to last, unlike so many of these modern monstrosities which I see arising these days; and it was well ordered. We had simple bentwood chairs with cane bottoms. No marble-topped tables with ball-fringed lace! No glass cabinets! I hung my treasured framed teaching diploma on the wall, with my religious pictures and some scenes of the English countryside. It was also my good fortune at this time to get an old autographed photograph of one of our first missionaries. In the decoration of our humble home my wife appeared to release all the energy and experience of her thirty-five years which had so far been denied expression.

To her, as to myself, everything came late. It was our fear, confirmed by the views of many friends who behind their expressions of goodwill concealed as we presently saw much uncharitableness, that we would be unable to have children, considering our advanced years. But they, and we, underestimated the power of prayer, for within a year of our marriage Winston was born.

The birth of Winston came to us as a grace and a blessing. Yet it also filled me with anxiety, for I could not refrain from assessing the difference between our ages. It occurred to me, for instance, that he would be thirty when I was eighty. It was a disturbing thought, for the companionship of children is something which, perhaps because of my profession, I hold especially dear. My anxiety had another reason. It was that Winston, in his most formative years, would be without not only my guidance – for what guidance can a man of seventy give to a lusty youngster of twenty? – but also without my financial support.

The problem of money, strange as it might appear, considering my unexpected elevation and all its accruing benefits, was occupying the minds of both my wife and myself. For my retirement was drawing near, and my pension would scarcely be more than what I subsisted on as a simple pupil teacher. It seemed then that like those pilgrims, whose enthusiasm I admire but cannot share, I was advancing towards my goal by taking two steps forward and one step back, though in my case a likelier simile might be that I was taking one step forward and one step back. So success always turns to ashes in the mouth of those who seek it as ardently as I had! And if I had the vision and the depth of faith which I now have, I might have seen even then how completely false are the things of this world, how much they flatter only to deceive.

We were both, as I say, made restless. And now the contemplation of baby Winston was a source of much pain to both of us, for the poor innocent creature could scarcely know what anguish awaited him when we would both be withdrawn from this vale of tears. His helplessness, his dependence tortured me. I was past the age when the taking out of an insurance policy was a practicable proposition; and during my days as a simple teacher I never had the resources to do so. It seemed, then, that I was being destroyed by my own good fortune, by the fruits of all my endeavour. Yet I did not heed this sign.

I continued while I could giving private lessons. I instituted a morning session as well, in addition to the afternoon one. But I did so with a heavy heart, tormented by the thought that in a few years this privilege and its small reward would be denied me, for private lessons, it must be understood, are considered the prerogative of a headmaster: in this way he stamps his character on the school. My results in the exhibition examinations for boys under twelve continued to be heartening; they far surpassed those of many other country schools. My religious zeal continued unabated; and it was this zeal which, burning in those years when most men in my position would have relaxed – they, fortunate souls, having their children fully grown – it was this surprising zeal, I say, which also contributed, I feel, to my later elevation which, as you will see from the plain narration of these events, I did not seek.

My retirement drew nearer. I became fiercer at school.

I wished all the boys under me could grow up at once. I was merciless towards the backward. My wife, poor creature, could not control her anxiety with as much success as myself. She had no occupation, no distracting vocation, in which her anxiety might have been consumed. She had only Winston, and this dear infant continually roused her to fears about his future. For his sake she would, I believe, have sacrificed her own life! It was not easy for her. And it required but the exercise of the mildest Christian charity to see that the reproaches she flung with increased acerbity and frequency at my head were but expressions of her anxiety. Sometimes, I must confess, I failed! And then my own unworthiness would torment me, as it torments me now.

We confided our problems to my wife's father, the schools inspector. Though we felt it unfair to let another partake of our troubles, it is none the less a recognized means of lightening any load which the individual finds too heavy to bear. But he, poor man, though as worried on his daughter's behalf as she was on Winston's, could offer only sympathy and little practical help. He reported that the authorities were unwilling to give me an extension of my tenure as headmaster. My despondency found expression in a display of temper, which he charitably forgave; for though he left the house, promising not to do another thing for us, he presently returned, and counselled patience.

So patient we were. I retired. I could hardly bear to remain at home, so used had I been to the daily round, the daily trials. I went out visiting, for no other reason than that I was afraid to be alone at home. My zeal, I believe, was remarked upon, though I took care to avoid the school, the scene of my late labours. I sought to take in for private lessons two or three pupils whose progress had deeply interested me. But my methods were no longer the methods that found favour! The parents of these children reported that the new headmaster had expressed himself strongly, and to my great disfavour, on the subject, to such a degree, in fact, that the progress of their children at school was being hampered, So I desisted; or rather, since the time has come for frankness, they left me.

The schools inspector, a regular visitor now at our humble, sad home, continued to counsel patience. I have so far refrained in this narrative from permitting my wife to speak directly; for I wish to do nothing that might increase the load she will surely have to bear, for my wife, though of considerable attainments, has not had the advantages of a formal education on which so much stress is nowadays laid. So I will refrain from chronicling the remark with which she greeted this advice of her father's. Suffice it to say that she spoke a children's rhyme without any great care for its metre or rhyme, the last of which indeed she destroyed by accidentally, in her haste, pulling down a vase from the centre-table on to the floor, where the water ran like one of the puddles which our baby Winston so lately made. After this incident relations between my wife and her father underwent a perceptible strain; and I took care to be out of the house as often as possible, and indeed it was pleasant to forget one's domestic troubles and walk abroad and be greeted as 'Headmaster' by the simple village folk.

Then, as it appears has happened so regularly throughout my life, the clouds rolled away and the sky brightened. I was appointed a School Manager. The announcement was made in the most heart-warming way possible, by the schools inspector himself, anticipating the official notification by a week or so. And the occasion became a family reunion. It was truly good to see the harassed schools inspector relaxing at last, and to see father and daughter reasonably happy with one another. My delight in this was almost as great as the delight in my new dignity.

For a school managership is a good thing to come to a man in the evening of his days. It permits an exercise of the most benign power imaginable. It permits a man at a speech day function to ask for a holiday for the pupils; and nothing is as warming as the lusty and sincere cheering that follows such a request. It gives power even over headmasters, for one can make surprise visits and it is in one's power to make reports to the authorities. It is a position of considerable responsibility as well, for a school manager manages a school as much as a managing director manages a company. It is in his power to decide whether the drains, say, need to be remade entirely or need simply be plastered over to look as new; whether one coat of paint or two are needed; whether a ceiling can be partially renovated and painted over or taken out altogether and replaced. He orders the number of desks and blackboards which he considers necessary, and the chalks and the stationery. It is, in short, a dignity ideally suited to one who has led an active life and is dismayed by the prospect of retirement. It brings honour as well as reward. It has the other advantage that school managers are like civil servants; they are seldom dismissed; and their honours tend to increase rather than diminish.

I entered on my new tasks with zeal, and once again all was well at our home. My wife's father visited us regularly, as though, poor man, anxious to share the good fortune for which he was to a large measure responsible. I looked after the school, the staff, the pupils. I visited all the parents of the pupils under my charge and spoke to them of the benefits of education, the dangers of absenteeism, and so on. I know I will be forgiven if I add that from time to time, whenever the ground appeared ripe, I sowed the seed of Presbyterianism or at any rate doubt among those who continued in the ways of darkness. Such zeal was unknown among school managers. I cannot account for it myself. It might be that my early austerity and ambition had given me something of the crusading zeal. But it was inevitable that such zeal should have been too much for some people to stomach.

For all his honour, for all the sweet cheers that greet his request for a holiday for the pupils, the school manager's position is one that sometimes attracts adverse and malicious comment. It is the fate of anyone who finds himself in a position of power and financial responsibility. The rumours persisted; and though they did not diminish the esteem in which I was so clearly held by the community – at the elections, for example, I was approached by all five candidates and asked to lend my voice to their cause, a situation of peculiar difficulty, which I resolved by promising all five to remain neutral, for which they were effusively grateful – it is no good thing for a man to walk among people who every day listen eagerly – for flesh is frail, and nothing attracts our simple villagers as much as scurrilous gossip – to slanders against himself. It was beneath my dignity, or rather, the dignity of my position, to reply to such attacks; and in this situation I turned, as I was turning with growing frequency, to my wife's father for advice. He suggested that I should relinquish one of my managerships, to indicate my disapproval of the gossip and the little esteem in which I held worldly honour. For I had so far succeeded in my new functions that I was now the manager of three schools, which was the maximum number permitted.

I followed his advice. I relinquished the managership of a school which was in a condition so derelict that not even repeated renovations could efface the original gimcrackery of its construction. This school had been the cause of most of the rumours, and my relinquishing of it attracted widespread comment and was even mentioned in the newspapers. It remained dear to me, but I was willing for it to go into other hands. This action of mine had the effect of stilling rumours and gossip. And the action proved to have its own reward, for some months later my wife's father, ever the bearer of good tidings, intimated that there was a possibility of a new school being put up in the area. I was thoroughly suited for its management; and he, the honest broker between the authorities and myself, said that my name was being mentioned in this connection. I was at that time manager of only two schools; I was entitled to a third. He warmly urged me to accept. I hesitated, and my hesitations were later proved to be justified. But the thought of a new school fashioned entirely according to my ideas and principles was too heady. I succumbed to temptation. If now I could only go back and withdraw that acceptance! The good man hurried back with the news; and within a fortnight I received the official notification.

I must confess that during the next few months I lost sight of my doubts in my zeal and enthusiasm for the new project. My two other schools suffered somewhat. For if there is a thing to delight the heart of the school manager, it is the management of a school not yet built. But, alas! We are at every step reminded of the vanity of worldly things. How often does it happen that a person, placed in the position he craves, a position which he is in every way suited to fill, suddenly loses his grip! Given the opportunity for which he longs, he is unable to make use of it. The effort goes all into the striving.

So now it happened with me. Nearly everything I touched failed to go as it should. I, so careful and correct in assessments and estimates, was now found repeatedly in error. None of my calculations were right. There were repeated shortages and stoppages. The school progressed far more slowly than I would have liked. And it was no consolation to me to find that in this moment I was alone, in this long moment of agony! Neither to my wife nor to her father could I turn for comfort. They savoured the joy of my managership of a new school without reference to me. I had my great opportunity; they had no doubt I would make use of it; and I could not bear disillusioning them or breaking into their happiness with my worries.

My errors attracted other errors. My errors multiplied, I tell you! To cover up one error I had to commit twenty acts of concealment, and these twenty had to be concealed. I felt myself caught in a curious inefficiency that seemed entirely beyond my control, something malignant, powered by forces hostile to myself. Until at length it seemed that failure was staring me in the face, and that my entire career would be forgotten in this crowning failure. The building went up, it is true. It had a respectable appearance. It looked a building. But it was far from what I had visualized. I had miscalculated badly, and it was too late to remedy the errors. Its faults, its weaknesses would be at once apparent even to the scantily trained eye. And now night after night I was tormented by this failure of mine. With the exercise of only a little judgment it could so easily have been made right. Yet now the time for that was past! Day after day I was drawn to the building, and every day I hoped that by some miracle it would have been effaced during the night. But there it always stood, a bitter reproach.

Matters were not made easier for me by the reproaches of my wife and her father. They both rounded on me and said with justice that my failure would involve them all. And the days went by! I could not – I have never liked bickering, the answering of insult with insult – I could not reproach them with having burdened me with such an enterprise at the end of my days. I did it for their glory, for I had acquired sufficient to last me until the end of my days. I did it for my wife and her father, and for my son Winston. But who will believe me? Who will believe that a man works for the glory of others, except he work for the glory of God? They reproached me. They stood aside from me. In this moment of need they deserted me.

They were bitter days. I went for long walks through our villages in the cool of the evening. The children ran out to greet me. Mothers looked up from their cooking, fathers from their perches on the roadside culverts, and greeted me, 'Headmaster!' And soon my failure would be apparent even to the humblest among them. I had to act quickly. Failures should be destroyed. The burning down of a school is an unforgiveable thing, but there are surely occasions when it can be condoned, when it is the only way out. Surely this was such an occasion! It is a drastic step. But it is one that has been taken more than once in this island. So I argued with myself. And always the answer was there: my failure had to be destroyed, not only for my own sake, but for the sake of all those, villagers included, whose fates were involved with mine.

Once I had made up my mind, I acted with decision. It was that time of year, mid-November, when people are beginning to think of Christmas to the exclusion of nearly everything else. This served my purpose well. I required – with what shame I now confess it – certain assistants, for it was necessary for me to be seen elsewhere on the day of the accident. Much money, much of what we had set aside for the future of our son Winston, had to go on this. And already it had been necessary to seal the lips of certain officials who had rejoiced in my failure and were willing to proclaim it to the world. But at last it was ready. On Boxing Day we would go to Port-of-Spain, to the races. When we returned the following day, the school would be no more. I say 'we', though my wife had not been apprised of my intentions.

With what fear, self-reproach, and self-disgust I waited for the days to pass! When I heard the Christmas carols, ever associated for me with the indefinable sweetness of Christmas Eve – which I now once more feel, thanks to my decision, though underneath there is a sense of doom and destruction, deserved, but with their own inevitable reward – when I heard carols and Christmas commercials on the radio, my heart sank; for it seemed that I had cut myself off from all about me, that once more I had become a stranger to the faith which I profess. So these days passed in sorrow, in nightly frenzies of prayer and self-castigation. Regret assailed me. Regret for what might have been, regret for what was to come. I was sinking, I felt, into a pit of defilement whence I could never emerge.

Of all this my wife knew nothing. But then she asked one day, 'What have you decided to do?' and, without waiting for my reply, at once drew up such a detailed plan, which corresponded so closely to what I had myself devised, that my heart quailed. For if, in this moment of my need, when the deepest resource was needed, I could devise a plan which might have been devised by anyone else, then discovery was certain. And to my shame, Winston, who only two or three days before had been teasing me with my previous unbaptized name, Winston took part in this discussion, with no appearance of shame on his face, only thrill and – sad am I to say it – a pride in me greater than I had ever seen the boy display.

How can one tell of the workings of the human heart? How can one speak of the urge to evil – an urge of which Christians more than anyone else are so aware – and of the countervailing urge to good? You must remember that this is the season of good will. And goodwill it was. For goodwill was what I was feeling towards all. At every carol my heart melted. Whenever a child rushed towards me and cried, 'Headmaster!' I was tormented by grief. For the sight of the unwashed creatures, deprived so many of them of schooling, which matters so much in those early years, and the absence of which ever afterwards makes itself felt, condemning a human being to an animal-like existence, the sight of these creatures, grateful towards me who had on so many evenings gone among them propagating the creed with what energy I could, unmanned me. They were proud of their new school. They were even prouder of their association with the man who had built it.

Everywhere I felt rejected. I went to church as often as I could, but even there I found rejection. And as the time drew nearer the enormity of what I proposed grew clearer to me. It was useless to tell myself that what I was proposing had been often done. The carols, the religious services, the talk of birth and life, they all unmanned me.

I walked among the children as one who had it in his power to provide or withhold blessing, and I thought of that other Walker, who said of those among whom I walked that they were blessed, and that theirs was the kingdom of heaven. And as I walked it seemed that at last I had seized the true essence of the religion I had adopted, and whose worldly success I had with such energy promoted. So that it seemed that these trials I was undergoing had been reserved to the end of my days, so that only then I could have a taste of the ecstasy about which I had so far only read. With this ecstasy I walked. It was Christmas Eve. It is Christmas Eve. My head felt drawn out of my body. I had difficulty in assessing the size and distance of objects. I felt myself tall. I felt myself part of the earth and yet removed.

And: 'No!' I said to my wife at teatime. 'No, I will not disgrace myself by this action of cowardice. Rather, I will proclaim my failure to the world and ask for my due punishment.'

She behaved as I expected. She had been busy putting up all sorts of Christmas decorations, expensive ones from the United States, which are all the rage now, so unlike the simple decorations I used to see in the homes of our early missionaries before the war. But how changed is the house to which we moved! How far has simplicity vanished and been replaced by show! And I gloried in it!

She begged me to change my mind. She summoned Winston to her help. They both wept and implored me to go through with our plan. But I was firm. I do believe that if the schools inspector were alive, he would also have been summoned to plead with me. But he, fortunate man, passed away some three weeks ago, entrusting his daughter and grandson to my care; and this alone is my fear, that by gaining glory for myself I might be injuring them. But I was firm. And then there started another of those scenes with which I had become only too familiar, and the house which that morning was filled with the enthusiasm of Winston was changed into one of mourning. Winston sobbed, tears running down his plump cheeks and down his well-shaped nose to his firm top lip, pleading with me to burn the school down, and generally behaving as though I had deprived him of a bonfire. And then a number of things were destroyed by his mother, and she left the house with Winston, vowing never to see me again, never to be involved in the disgrace which was sure to come.

And so here I sit, waiting not for Christmas, but in this house where the autographed photograph of one of our earliest missionaries gazes down at me through his rich beard and luxuriant eyebrows, and where the walls carry so many reminders of my past life of endeavour and hardship and struggle and triumph and also, alas, final failure, I wait for the day after Boxing Day, after the races to which we were to have gone, for the visit of the inspectors of the Audit Department. The house is lonely and dark. The radios play the Christmas songs. I am very lonely. But I am strong. And here I lay down my pen. My hand tires; the beautiful letters we were taught to fashion at the mission school have begun to weaken and to straggle untidily over the ruled paper; and someone is knocking.

December 27. How can one speak of the ways of the world, how can one speak of the tribulations that come one's way? Even expiation is denied me. For even as I wrote the last sentence of the above account, there came a knocking at my door, and I went to open unto him who knocked. And lo, there was a boy, bearing tidings. And behold, towards the west the sky had reddened, and the boy informed me that the school was ablaze. What could I do? My world fell about my ears. Even final expiation, final triumph, it seemed, was denied me. Certain things are not for me. In this moment of anguish and despair my first thought was for my wife. Where had she gone? I went out to seek her. When I returned, after a fruitless errand, I discovered that she and Winston had come back to seek me. Smiling through our tears, we embraced. So it was Christmas after all for us. And, with lightened heart, made heavy only by my wrestling with the Lord, we went to the races on Boxing Day, yesterday. We did not gamble. It is against our principles. The inspectors from the Audit Department sent word today that they would not, after all, come.

1962

The Mourners

I walked up the back stairs into the veranda white in the afternoon sun. I could never bring myself to enter that house by the front stairs. We were poor relations; we had been taught to respect the house and the family.

On the right of the veranda was the kitchen, tiled and spruce and with every modern gadget. An ugly Indian girl with a pockmarked face and slack breasts was washing some dishes. She wore a dirty red print frock.

When she saw me she said, 'Hello, Romesh.' She had opened brightly but ended on a subdued tone that was more suitable.

'Hello,' I said softly. 'Is she there?' I jerked my thumb towards the drawing-room that lay straight ahead.

'Yes. Boy, she cries all day. And the baby was so cute too.' The servant girl was adapting herself to the language of the house.

'Can I go in now?'

'Yes,' she whispered. Drying her hands on her frock, she led the way. Her kitchen was clean and pure, but all the impurities seemed to have stuck on her. She tiptoed to the jalousied door, opened it an inch or two, peered in deferentially and said in a louder voice, 'Romesh here, Miss Sheila.'

There was a sigh inside. The girl opened the door and shut it behind me. The curtains had been drawn all around. The room was full of a hot darkness smelling of ammonia and oil. Through the ventilation slits some light came into the room, enough to make Sheila distinct. She was in a loose lemon housecoat; she half sat, half reclined on a pink sofa.

I walked across the polished floor as slowly and silently as I could. I shifted my eyes from Sheila to the table next to the sofa. I didn't know how to begin.

It was Sheila who broke the silence. She looked me up and down in the half-light and said, 'My, Romesh, you are growing up.' She smiled with tears in her eyes. 'How are you? And your mother?'

Sheila didn't like my mother. 'They're all well – all at home are well,' I said. 'And how are you?'

She managed a little laugh. 'Still *living*. Pull up a chair. No, no – not yet. Let me look at you. My, you are getting to be a handsome young man.'

I pulled up a chair and sat down. I sat with my legs wide apart at first. But this struck me as being irreverent and too casual. So I put my knees together and let my hands rest loosely on them. I sat upright. Then I looked at Sheila. She smiled.

Then she began to cry. She reached for the damp handkerchief on the table. I got up and asked whether she would like the smelling salts or the bay rum. Jerking with sobs, she shook her head and told me, in words truncated by tears, to sit down.

I sat still, not knowing what to do.

With the handkerchief she wiped her eyes, pulled out a larger handkerchief from her housecoat and blew her nose. Then she smiled. 'You must forgive me for breaking down like this,' she said.

I was going to say, 'That's all right,' but the words felt too free. So I opened my mouth and made an unintelligible noise.

'You never knew my son, Romesh?'

'I only saw him once,' I lied; and instantly regretted the lie. Suppose she asked me where I had seen him or when I had seen him. In fact, I never knew that Sheila's baby was a boy until he died and the news spread.

But she wasn't going to examine me. 'I have some pictures of him.' She called in a gentle, strained voice: 'Soomintra.'

The servant girl opened the door. 'You want something, Miss Sheila?'

'Yes, Soomin,' Sheila said (and I noticed that she had shortened the girl's name, a thing that was ordinarily not done). 'Yes, I want the snapshots of Ravi.' At the name she almost burst into tears, but flung her head back at the last moment and smiled.

When Soomintra left the room I looked at the walls. In the dim light I could make out an engraving of the Princes in the Tower, a print of a stream lazing bluely beautiful through banks cushioned with flowers. I was looking at the walls to escape looking at Sheila. But her eyes followed mine and rested on the Princes in the Tower.

'You know the story?' she asked.

'Yes.'

'Look at them. They're going to be killed, you know. It's only in the past two days I've really got to understand that picture, you know. The boys. So sad. And look at the dog. Not understanding a thing. Just wanting to get out.'

'It is a sad picture.'

She brushed a tear from her eye and smiled once more. 'But tell me, Romesh, how are you getting on with your studies?'

'As usual.'

'Are you going away?'

'If I do well in the exams.'

'But you're bound to do well. After all, your father is no fool.'

It seemed overbearingly selfish to continue listening. I said, 'You needn't talk, if you don't want to.'

Soomintra brought the snapshot album. It was an expensive album, covered in leather. Ravi had been constantly photographed, from the time he had been allowed into the open air to the month before his death. There were pictures of him in bathing costume, digging sand on the east coast, the north coast and the south coast; pictures of Ravi dressed up for Carnival, dressed up for tea parties; Ravi on tricycles, Ravi in motor-cars, real ones and toy ones; Ravi in the

company of scores of people I didn't know. I turned the pages
with due lassitude. From time to time Sheila leaned forward
and commented. 'There's Ravi at the home of that American
doctor. A wunnerful guy. He looks sweet, doesn't he? And
look at this one: that boy always had a smile for the camera.
He always knew what we were doing. He was a very smart
little kid.'

At last we exhausted the snapshots. Sheila had grown
silent towards the end. I felt she had been through the
album many times in the past two days.

I tapped my hands on my knees. I looked at the clock on
the wall and the Princes in the Tower. Sheila came to the
rescue. 'I am sure you are hungry.'

I shook my head faintly.

'Soomin will fix something for you.'

Soomintra did prepare something for me, and I ate in the
kitchen – their food was always good. I prepared to face the
farewell tears and smiles. But just then the Doctor came. He
was Sheila's husband and everyone knew him as 'The Doctor'. He was tall with a pale handsome face that now looked
drawn and tired.

'Hello, Romesh.'

'Hello, Doctor.'

'How is she?'

'Not very happy.'

'She'll be all right in a couple of days. The shock, you
know. And she's a very delicate girl.'

'I hope she gets over it soon.'

He smiled and patted me on the shoulder. He pulled the
blinds to shut out the sun from the veranda, and made me sit
down.

'You knew my son?'

'Only slightly.'

'He was a fine child. We wanted – or rather, I wanted – to
enter him in the Cow and Gate Baby Contest. But Sheila
didn't care for the idea.'

I could find nothing to say.

'When he was four he used to sing, you know. All sorts of songs. In English and Hindi. You know that song – *I'll Be Seeing You?*'

I nodded.

'He used to sing that through and through. He had picked up all the words. Where from I don't know, but he'd picked them up. And even now I don't know half the words myself. He was like that. Quick. And do you know the last words he said to me were "I'll be seeing you in all the old familiar places"? When Sheila heard that he was dead she looked at me and began to cry. "I'll be seeing you," she said.'

I didn't look at him.

'It makes you think, doesn't it? Makes you think about life. Here today. Gone tomorrow. It makes you think about life and death, doesn't it? But here I go, philosophizing again. Why don't you start giving lessons to children?' he asked me abruptly. 'You could make tons of money that way. I know a boy who's making fifty dollars a month by giving lessons one afternoon a week.'

'I am busy with my exams.'

He paid no attention. 'Tell me, have you seen the pictures we took of Ravi last Carnival?'

I hadn't the heart to say yes.

'Soomin,' he called, 'bring the photograph album.'

1950

The Night Watchman's
Occurrence Book

November 21. 10.30 p.m. C. A. Cavander take over duty at C—— Hotel all corrected. *Cesar Alwyn Cavander*

7 a.m. C. A. Cavander hand over duty to Mr Vignales at C—— Hotel no report. *Cesar Alwyn Cavander*

November 22. 10.30 p.m. C. A. Cavander take over duty at C—— Hotel no report. *Cesar Alwyn Cavander*

7 a.m. C. A. Cavander hand over duty to Mr Vignales at C—— Hotel all corrected. *Cesar Alwyn Cavander*

This is the third occasion on which I have found C. A. Cavander, Night Watchman, asleep on duty. Last night, at 12.45 a.m., I found him sound asleep in a rocking chair in the hotel lounge. Night Watchman Cavander has therefore been dismissed.

Night Watchman Hillyard: This book is to be known in future as 'The Night Watchman's Occurrence Book'. In it I shall expect to find a detailed account of everything that happens in the hotel tonight. Be warned by the example of ex-Night Watchman Cavander. *W. A. G. Inskip, Manager*

Mr Manager, remarks noted. You have no worry where I am concern sir. *Charles Ethelbert Hillyard, Night Watchman*

November 23. 11 p.m. Night Watchman Hillyard take over duty at C—— Hotel with one torch light 2 fridge keys and room keys 1, 3, 6, 10 and 13. Also 25 cartoons Carib Beer and 7 cartoons Heineken and 2 cartoons American cigarettes. Beer cartoons intact Bar intact all corrected no report. *Charles Ethelbert Hillyard*

7 a.m. Night Watchman Hillyard hand over duty to Mr Vignales at C—— Hotel with one torch light 2 fridge keys and room keys, 1, 3, 6, 10 and 13. 32 cartoons beer. Bar intact all corrected no report. *Charles Ethelbert Hillyard*

> Night Watchman Hillyard: Mr Wills complained bitterly to me this morning that last night he was denied entry to the bar by you. I wonder if you know exactly what the purpose of this hotel is. In future all hotel guests are to be allowed entry to the bar at whatever time they choose. It is your duty simply to note what they take. This is one reason why the hotel provides a certain number of beer cartons (please note the spelling of this word). *W. A. G. Inskip*

Mr Manager, remarks noted. I sorry I didnt get the chance to take some education sir. *Chas. Ethelbert Hillyard*

November 24. 11 p.m. N.W. Hillyard take over duty with one Torch, 1 Bar Key, 2 Fridge Keys, 32 cartoons Beer, all intact. 12 Midnight Bar close and Barman left leaving Mr Wills and others in Bar, and they left at 1 a.m. Mr Wills took 16 Carib Beer, Mr Wilson 8, Mr Percy 8. At 2 a.m. Mr Wills come back in the bar and take 4 Carib and some bread, he cut his hand trying to cut the bread, so please dont worry about the stains on the carpet sir. At 6 a.m. Mr Wills come back for some soda water. It didn't have any so he take a ginger beer instead. Sir you see it is my intention to do this job good sir, I cant see how Night Watchman Cavander could fall asleep on this job sir. *Chas. Ethelbert Hillyard*

> You always seems sure of the time, and guests appear to be in the habit of entering the bar on the hour. You will kindly note the exact time. The clock from the kitchen is left on the window near the switches. You can use this

clock but you MUST replace it every morning before you go off duty. *W. A. G. Inskip*

Noted. *Chas. Ethelbert Hillyard*

November 25. Midnight Bar close and 12.23 a.m. Barman left leaving Mr Wills and others in Bar. Mr Owen take 5 bottles Carib, Mr Wilson 6 bottles Heineken, Mr Wills 18 Carib and they left at 2.52 a.m. Nothing unusual. Mr Wills was helpless, I don't see how anybody could drink so much, eighteen one man alone, this work enough to turn anybody Seventh Day Adventist, and another man come in the bar, I dont know his name, I hear they call him Paul, he assist me because the others couldn't do much, and we take Mr Wills up to his room and take off his boots and slack his other clothes and then we left. Don't know sir if they did take more while I was away, nothing was mark on the Pepsi Cola board, but they was drinking still, it look as if they come back and take some more, but with Mr Wills I want some extra assistance sir.

Mr Manager, the clock break I find it break when I come back from Mr Wills room sir. It stop 3.19 sir. *Chas. E. Hillyard*

> More than 2 lbs of veal were removed from the Fridge last night, and a cake that was left in the press was cut. It is your duty, Night Watchman Hillyard, to keep an eye on these things. I ought to warn you that I have also asked the Police to check on all employees leaving the hotel, to prevent such occurrences in the future. *W. A. G. Inskip*

Mr Manager, I don't know why people so anxious to blame servants sir. About the cake, the press lock at night and I dont have the key sir, everything safe where I am concern sir. *Chas. Hillyard*

November 26. Midnight Bar close and Barman left. Mr Wills

didn't come, I hear he at the American base tonight, all quiet, nothing unusual.

Mr Manager, I request one thing. Please inform the Barman to let me know sir when there is a female guest in the hotel sir. *C. E. Hillyard*

> This morning I received a report from a guest that there were screams in the hotel during the night. You wrote All Quiet. Kindly explain in writing. *W. A. G. Inskip*
> Write Explanation here:

EXPLANATION. Not long after midnight the telephone ring and a woman ask for Mr Jimminez. I try to tell her where he was but she say she cant hear properly. Fifteen minutes later she came in a car, she was looking vex and sleepy, and I went up to call him. The door was not lock, I went in and touch his foot and call him very soft, and he jump up and begin to shout. When he come to himself he said he had Night Mere, and then he come down and went away with the woman, was not necessary to mention.

Mr Manager, I request you again, please inform the Barman to let me know sir when there is a female guest in the hotel. *C. Hillyard*

November 27. 1 a.m. Bar close, Mr Wills and a American 19 Carib and 2.30 a.m. a Police come and ask for Mr Wills, he say the American report that he was robbed of $200.00¢, he was last drinking at the C—— with Mr Wills and others. Mr Wills and the Police ask to open the Bar to search it, I told them I cannot open the Bar for you like that, the Police must come with the Manager. Then the American say it was only joke he was joking, and they try to get the Police to laugh, but the Police looking the way I feeling. Then laughing Mr Wills left in a garage car as he couldn't drive himself and the American was waiting outside and they both fall down as they was getting in the car, and Mr Wills saying any time you want a overdraft you just come to my bank kiddo. The Police left walking by himself. *C. Hillyard*

Night Watchman Hillyard: 'Was not necessary to mention'!! You are not to decide what is necessary to mention in this night watchman's occurrence book. Since when have you become sole owner of the hotel as to determine what is necessary to mention? If the guest did not mention it I would never have known that there were screams in the hotel during the night. Also will you kindly tell me who Mr Jimminez is? And what rooms he occupied or occupies? And by what right? You have been told by me personally that the names of all hotel guests are on the slate next to the light switches. If you find Mr Jimminez's name on this slate, or could give me some information about him, I will be most warmly obliged to you. The lady you ask about is Mrs Roscoe, Room 12, as you very well know. It is your duty to see that guests are not pestered by unauthorized callers. You should give no information about guests to such people, and I would be glad if in future you could direct such callers straight to me. *W. A. G. Inskip*

Sir was what I ask you two times, I dont know what sort of work I take up, I always believe that nightwatchman work is a quiet work and I dont like meddling in white people business, but the gentleman occupy Room 12 also, was there that I went up to call him, I didn't think it necessary to mention because was none of my business sir. *C.E.H.*

November 28. 12 Midnight Bar close and Barman left at 12.20 a.m. leaving Mr Wills and others, and they all left at 1.25 a.m. Mr Wills 8 Carib, Mr Wilson 12, Mr Percy 8, and the man they call Paul 12. Mrs Roscoe join the gentlemen at 12.33 a.m., four gins, everybody calling her Minnie from Trinidad, and then they start singing that song, and some others. Nothing unusual. Afterwards there were mild singing and guitar music in Room 12. A man come in and ask to use the phone at 2.17 a.m. and while he was using it about 7 men come in and wanted to beat him up, so he put down the phone and they all ran away. At 3 a.m. I notice the padlock not on the press, I look inside, no cake, but the padlock was not put on in the first place sir. Mr Wills come down again at 6 a.m. to look for his sweet, he look in the Fridge and did not see any. He took a piece of pineapple. A plate was covered in the Fridge, but it didn't have anything in it. Mr Wills put it out, the cat jump on it and it fall down and break. The garage bulb not burning. *C.E.H.*

You will please sign your name at the bottom of your report. You are in the habit of writing Nothing Unusual. Please take note and think before making such a statement. I want to know what is meant by nothing unusual. I gather, not from you, needless to say, that the police have fallen into the habit of visiting the hotel at night. I would be most grateful to you if you could find the time to note the times of these visits. *W. A. G. Inskip*

Sir, nothing unusual means everything usual. I dont know, nothing I writing you liking. I don't know what sort of work this night watchman work getting to be, since when people have to start getting Cambridge certificate to get night watchman job, I ain't educated and because of this everybody think they could insult me. *Charles Ethelbert Hillyard*

November 29. Midnight Bar close and 12.15 Barman left leaving Mr Wills and Mrs Roscoe and others in the Bar. Mr Wills and Mrs Roscoe left at 12.30 a.m. leaving Mr Wilson and the man they call Paul, and they all left at 1.00 a.m. Twenty minutes to 2 Mr Wills and party return and left again at 5 to 3. At 3.45 Mr Wills return and take bread and milk and olives and cherries, he ask for nutmeg too, I said we had none, he drink 2 Carib, and left ten minutes later. He also collect Mrs Roscoe bag. All the drinks, except the 2 Carib, was taken by the man they call Paul. I don't know sir I don't like this sort of work, you better hire a night barman. At 5.30 Mrs Roscoe and the man they call Paul come back to the bar, they was having a quarrel, Mr Paul saying you make me sick, Mrs Roscoe saying I feel sick, and then she vomit all over the floor, shouting I didn't want that damned milk. I was cleaning up when Mr Wills come down to ask for soda water, we got to lay in more soda for Mr Wills, but I need extra assistance with Mr Wills Paul and party sir.

The police come at 2, 3.48 and 4.52. They sit down in the bar a long time. Firearms discharge 2 times in the back yard. Detective making inquiries. I dont know sir, I thinking it would be better for me to go back to some other sort of job. At 3 I hear somebody shout Thief, and I see a man running out of the back, and Mr London, Room 9, say he miss 80 cents and a pack of cigarettes which was on his dressing case. I don't know when the people in this place does sleep. *Chas. Ethelbert Hillyard*

> Night Watchman Hillyard: A lot more than 80 cents was stolen. Several rooms were in fact entered during the night, including my own. You are employed to prevent such things occurring. Your interest in the morals of our guests seems to be distracting your attention from your duties. Save your preaching for your roadside prayer meetings. Mr Pick, Room 7, reports that in spite of the most pressing and repeated requests, you did not awaken him at 5. He has missed his plane to British Guiana as a result. No newspapers were delivered to the rooms this morning. I am again notifying you that papers must be handed personally to Doorman Vignales. And the messenger's bicycle, which I must remind you is the property of the hotel, has been damaged. What do you *do* at nights? *W. A. G. Inskip*

Please don't ask me sir.

Relating to the damaged bicycle: I left the bicycle the same place where I meet it, nothing took place so as to damage it. I always take care of all property sir. I don't know how you could think I have time to go out for bicycle rides. About the papers, sir, the police and them read it and

leave them in such a state that I didn't think it would be nice
to give them to guests. I wake up Mr Pick, room 7, at
4.50 a.m. 5 a.m. 5.15 a.m. and 5.30. He told me to keep off,
he would not get up, and one time he pelt a box of matches
at me, matches scatter all over the place. I always do everything to the best of my ability sir but God is my Witness I
never find a night watchman work like this, so much writing
I dont have time to do anything else, I dont have four hands
and six eyes and I want this extra assistance with Mr Wills
and party sir. I am a poor man and you could abuse me, but
you must not abuse my religion sir because the good Lord
sees All and will have His revenge sir, I don't know what
sort of work and trouble I land myself in, all I want is a
little quiet night work and all I getting is abuse. *Chas. E.
Hillyard*

November 30. 12.25 a.m. Bar close and Barman left 1.00 a.m.
leaving Mr Wills and party in Bar. Mr Wills take 12 Carib,
Mr Wilson 6, Mr Percy 14. Mrs Roscoe five gins. At 1.30
a.m. Mrs Roscoe left and there were a little singing and mild
guitar playing in Room 12. Nothing unusual. The police
came at 1.35 and sit down in the bar for a time, not drinking,
not talking, not doing anything except watching. At 1.45 the
man they call Paul come in with Mr McPherson of the SS
Naparoni, they was both falling down and laughing whenever
anything break and the man they call Paul say Fireworks
about to begin tell Minnie Malcolm coming the ship just
dock. Mr Wills and party scatter leaving one or two bottles
half empty and then the man they call Paul tell me to go up
to Room 12 and tell Minnie Roscoe that Malcolm coming.
I don't know how people could behave so the thing enough to
make anybody turn priest. I notice the padlock on the bar
door break off it hanging on only by a little piece of wood.
And when I went up to Room 12 and tell Mrs Roscoe that
Malcolm coming the ship just dock the woman get sober
straight away like she dont want to hear no more guitar
music and she asking me where to hide where to go. I dont

know, I feel the day of reckoning is at hand, but she not listening to what I saying, she busy straightening up the room one minute packing the next, and then she run out into the corridor and before I could stop she she run straight down the back stairs to the annexe. And then 5 past 2, still in the corridor, I see a big red man running up to me and he sober as a judge and he mad as a drunkard and he asking me where she is where she is. I ask whether he is a authorized caller, he say you don't give me any of that crap now, where she is, where she is. So remembering about the last time and Mr Jimminez I direct him to the manager office in the annexe. He hear a little scuffling inside Mr Inskip room and I make out Mr Inskip sleepy voice and Mrs Roscoe voice and the red man run inside and all I hearing for the next five minutes is bam bam bodow bodow bow and this woman screaming. I dont know what sort of work this night watchman getting I want something quiet like the police. In time things quiet down and the red man drag Mrs Roscoe out of the annexe and they take a taxi, and the Police sitting down quiet in the bar. Then Mr Percy and the others come back one by one to the bar and they talking quiet and they not drinking and they left 3 a.m. 3.15 Mr Wills return and take one whisky and 2 Carib. He asked for pineapple or some sweet fruit but it had nothing.

6 a.m. Mr Wills come in the bar looking for soda but it aint have none. We have to get some soda for Mr Wills sir.

6.30 a.m. the papers come and I deliver them to Doorman Vignales at 7 a.m. *Chas. Hillyard*

Mr Hillyard: In view of the unfortunate illness of Mr Inskip, I am temporarily in charge of the hotel. I trust you will continue to make your nightly reports, but I would be glad if you could keep your entries as brief as possible. *Robt. Magnus, Acting Manager*

December 1. 10.30 p.m. C. E. Hillyard take over duty at C—— Hotel all corrected 12 Midnight Bar close 2 a.m.

Mr Wills 2 Carib, 1 bread 6 a.m. Mr Wills 1 soda 7 a.m. Night Watchman Hillyard hand over duty to Mr Vignales with one torch light 2 Fridge keys and Room Keys 1, 3, 6 and 12. Bar intact all corrected no report. *C.E.H.*

1962

The Enemy

I had always considered this woman, my mother, as the
enemy. She was sure to misunderstand anything I did, and
the time came when I thought she not only misunderstood
me, but quite definitely disapproved of me. I was an only
child, but for her I was one too many.

She hated my father, and even after he died she continued
to hate him.

She would say, 'Go ahead and do what you doing. You
is your father child, you hear, not mine.'

The real split between my mother and me happened not
in Miguel Street, but in the country.

My mother had decided to leave my father, and she
wanted to take me to her mother.

I refused to go.

My father was ill, and in bed. Besides, he had promised
that if I stayed with him I was to have a whole box of
crayons.

I chose the crayons and my father.

We were living at the time in Cunupia, where my father
was a driver on the sugar estates. He wasn't a slave-driver,
but a driver of free people, but my father used to behave as
though the people were slaves. He rode about the estates
on a big clumsy brown horse, cracking his whip at the
labourers and people said – I really don't believe this – that
he used to kick the labourers.

I don't believe it because my father had lived all his life
in Cunupia and he knew that you really couldn't push the
Cunupia people around. They are not tough people, but they

think nothing of killing, and they are prepared to wait years for the chance to kill someone they don't like. In fact, Cunupia and Tableland are the two parts of Trinidad where murders occur often enough to ensure quick promotion for the policemen stationed there.

At first we lived in the barracks, but then my father wanted to move to a little wooden house not far away.

My mother said, 'You playing hero. Go and live in your house by yourself, you hear.'

She was afraid, of course, but my father insisted. So we moved to the house, and then trouble really started.

A man came to the house one day about midday and said to my mother, 'Where your husband?'

My mother said, 'I don't know.'

The man was cleaning his teeth with a twig from a hibiscus plant. He spat and said, 'It don't matter. I have time. I could wait.'

My mother said, 'You ain't doing nothing like that. I know what you thinking, but I have my sister coming here right now.'

The man laughed and said, 'I not doing anything. I just want to know when he coming home.'

I began to cry in terror.

The man laughed.

My mother said, 'Shut up this minute or I give you something really to cry about.'

I went to another room and walked about saying, 'Rama! Rama! Sita Rama!' This was what my father had told me to say when I was in danger of any sort.

I looked out of the window. It was bright daylight, and hot, and there was nobody else in all the wide world of bush and trees.

And then I saw my aunt walking up the road.

She came and she said, 'Anything wrong with you here? I was at home just sitting quite quiet, and I suddenly feel that something was going wrong. I feel I had to come to see.'

The man said, 'Yes, I know the feeling.'

My mother, who was being very brave all the time, began to cry.

But all this was only to frighten us, and we were certainly frightened. My father always afterwards took his gun with him, and my mother kept a sharpened cutlass by her hand.

Then, at night, there used to be voices, sometimes from the road, sometimes from the bushes behind the house. The voices came from people who had lost their way and wanted lights, people who had come to tell my father that his sister had died suddenly in Debe, people who had come just to tell my father that there was a big fire at the sugar-mill. Sometimes there would be two or three of these voices, speaking from different directions, and we would sit awake in the dark house, just waiting, waiting for the voices to fall silent. And when they did fall silent it was even more terrible.

My father used to say, 'They still outside. They want you to go out and look.'

And at four or five o'clock when the morning light was coming up we would hear the tramp of feet in the bush, feet going away.

As soon as darkness fell we would lock ourselves up in the house, and wait. For days there would sometimes be nothing at all, and then we would hear them again.

My father brought home a dog one day. We called it Tarzan. He was more of a playful dog than a watch-dog, a big hairy brown dog, and I would ride on its back.

When evening came I said, 'Tarzan coming in with us?'

He wasn't. He remained whining outside the door, scratching it with his paws.

Tarzan didn't last long.

One morning we found him hacked to pieces and flung on the top step.

We hadn't heard any noise the night before.

My mother began to quarrel with my father, but my father was behaving as though he didn't really care what happened to him or to any of us.

My mother used to say, 'You playing brave. But bravery

ain't going to give any of us life, you hear. Let us leave this place.'

My father began hanging up words of hope on the walls of the house, things from the Gita and the Bible, and sometimes things he had just made up.

He also lost his temper more often with my mother, and the time came when as soon as she entered a room he would scream and pelt things at her.

So she went back to her mother and I remained with my father.

During those days my father spent a lot of his time in bed, and so I had to lie down with him. For the first time I really talked to my father. He taught me three things.

The first was this.

'Boy,' my father asked, 'Who is your father?'

I said, 'You is my father.'

'Wrong.'

'How that wrong?'

My father said, 'You want to know who your father really is? God is your father.'

'And what you is, then?'

'Me, what I is? I is – let me see, well, I is just a second sort of father, not your real father.'

This teaching was later to get me into trouble, particularly with my mother.

The second thing my father taught me was the law of gravity.

We were sitting on the edge of the bed, and he dropped the box of matches.

He asked, 'Now, boy, tell me why the matches drop.'

I said, 'But they bound to drop. What you want them to do? Go sideways?'

My father said, 'I will tell why they drop. They drop because of the laws of gravity.'

And he showed me a trick. He half filled a bucket with water and spun the bucket fast over his shoulder.

He said, 'Look, the water wouldn't fall.'

But it did. He got a soaking and the floor was wet.

He said, 'It don't matter. I just put too much water, that's all. Look again.'

The second time it worked.

The third thing my father taught me was the blending of colours. This was just a few days before he died. He was very ill, and he used to spend a lot of time shivering and mumbling; and even when he fell asleep I used to hear him groaning.

I remained with him on the bed most of the time.

He said to me one day, 'You got the coloured pencils?'

I took them from under the pillow.

He said, 'You want to see some magic?'

I said, 'What, you know magic really?'

He took the yellow pencil and filled in a yellow square.

He asked, 'Boy, what colour this is?'

I said, 'Yellow.'

He said, 'Just pass me the blue pencil now, and shut your eyes tight tight.'

When I opened my eyes he said, 'Boy, what colour this square is now?'

I said, 'You sure you ain't cheating?'

He laughed and showed me how blue and yellow make green.

I said, 'You mean if I take a leaf and wash it and wash it and wash it really good, it go be yellow or blue when I finish with it?'

He said, 'No. You see, is God who blend those colours. God, your father.'

I spent a lot of my time trying to make up tricks. The only one I could do was to put two match-heads together, light them, and make them stick. But my father knew that. But at last I found a trick that I was sure my father didn't know. He never got to know about it because he died on the night I was to show it him.

It had been a day of great heat, and in the afternoon the sky had grown low and heavy and black. It felt almost chilly in the house, and my father was sitting wrapped up in the rocking chair. The rain began to fall drop by heavy drop, beating like a hundred fists on the roof. It grew dark and I lit the oil lamp, sticking in a pin in the wick, to keep away bad spirits from the house.

My father suddenly stopped rocking and whispered, 'Boy, they here tonight. Listen. Listen.'

We were both silent and I listened carefully, but my ears could catch nothing but the wind and the rain.

A window banged itself open. The wind whooshed in with heavy raindrops.

'God!' my father screamed.

I went to the window. It was a pitch black night, and the world was a wild and lonely place, with only the wind and the rain on the leaves. I had to fight to pull the window in, and before I could close it, I saw the sky light up with a crack of lightning.

I shut the window and waited for the thunder.

It sounded like a steamroller on the roof.

My father said, 'Boy, don't frighten. Say what I tell you to say.'

I went and sat at the foot of the rocking chair and I began to say, 'Rama! Rama! Sita Rama!'

My father joined in. He was shivering with cold and fright.

Suddenly he shouted, 'Boy, they here. They here. I hear them talking under the house. They could do what they like in all this noise and nobody could hear them.'

I said, 'Don't fraid, I have this cutlass here, and you have your gun.'

But my father wasn't listening.

He said, 'But it dark, man. It so dark. It so dark.'

I got up and went to the table for the oil lamp to bring it nearer. But just then there was an explosion of thunder so low it might have been just above the roof. It rolled and rumbled for a long long time. Then another window blew open and the oil lamp was blown out. The wind and the rain tore into the dark room.

My father screamed out once more, 'Oh God, it dark.'

I was lost in a black world. I screamed until the thunder died away and the rain had become a drizzle. I forgot all about the trick I had prepared for my father: the soap I had rubbed into the palms of my hands until it had dried and disappeared.

Everybody agreed on one thing. My mother and I had to leave the country. Port-of-Spain was the safest place. There was too a lot of laughter against my father, and it appeared that for the rest of my life I would have to bear the cross of a father who died from fright. But in a month or so I had forgotten my father, and I had begun to look upon myself as the boy who had no father. It seemed natural.

In fact, when we moved to Port-of-Spain and I saw what the normal relationship between father and son was – it was nothing more than the relationship between the beater and the beaten – when I saw this I was grateful.

My mother made a great thing at first about keeping me in my place and knocking out all the nonsense my father had taught me. I don't know why she didn't try harder, but the fact is that she soon lost interest in me, and she let me run about the street, only rushing down to beat me from time to time.

Occasionally, though, she would take the old firm line.

One day she kept me home. She said, 'No school for you today. I just sick of tying your shoe-laces for you. Today you go have to learn that!'

I didn't think she was being fair. After all, in the country none of us wore shoes and I wasn't used to them.

That day she beat me and beat me and made me tie knot after knot and in the end I still couldn't tie my shoelaces. For years afterwards it was a great shame to me that I couldn't do a simple thing like that, just as how I couldn't peel an orange. But about the shoes I made up a little trick. I never made my mother buy shoes the correct size. I pretended that those shoes hurt, and I made her get me shoes a

size or two bigger. Once the attendant had tied the laces up
for me, I never undid them, and I merely slipped my feet in
and out of the shoes. To keep them on my feet, I stuck paper
in the toes.

To hear my mother talk, you would think I was a freak.
Nearly every little boy she knew was better and more intelligent. There was one boy she knew who helped his mother
paint her house. There was another boy who could mend his
own shoes. There was still another boy who at the age of
thirteen was earning a good twenty dollars a month, while
I was just idling and living off her blood.

Still, there were surprising glimpses of kindness.

There was the time, for instance, when I was cleaning
some tumblers for her one Saturday morning. I dropped a
tumbler and it broke. Before I could do anything about it my
mother saw what had happened.

She said, 'How you break it?'

I said, 'It just slip off. It smooth smooth.'

She said, 'Is a lot of nonsense drinking from glass. They
break up so easy.'

And that was all. I got worried about my mother's health.
She was never worried about mine.

She thought that there was no illness in the world a stiff
dose of hot Epsom Salts couldn't cure. That was a penance I
had to endure once a month. It completely ruined my week-
end. And if there was something she couldn't understand,
she sent me to the Health Office in Tragarete Road. That was
an awful place. You waited and waited and waited before you
went in to see the doctor.

Before you had time to say, 'Doctor, I have a pain – ' he
would be writing out a prescription for you. And again you
had to wait for the medicine. All the Health Office medicines
were the same. Water and a pink sediment half an inch thick.

Hat used to say of the Health Office, 'The Government
take up faith healing.'

My mother considered the Health Office a good place for
me to go to. I would go there at eight in morning and return

any time after two in the afternoon. It kept me out of mischief, and it cost only twenty-four cents a year.

But you mustn't get the impression that I was a saint all the time. I wasn't. I used to have odd fits where I just couldn't take an order from anybody, particularly my mother. I used to feel that I would dishonour myself for life if I took anybody's orders. And life is a funny thing, really. I sometimes got these fits just when my mother was anxious to be nice to me.

The day after Hat rescued me from drowning at Dockside I wrote an essay for my schoolmaster on the subject, 'A Day at the Seaside'. I don't think any schoolmaster ever got an essay like that. I talked about how I was nearly drowned and how calmly I was facing death, with my mind absolutely calm, thinking, 'Well, boy, this is the end.' The teacher was so pleased he gave me ten marks out of twelve.

He said, 'I think you are a genius.'

When I went home I told my mother, 'That essay I write today, I get ten out of twelve for it.'

My mother said, 'How you so bold-face to lie brave brave so in front of my face? You want me give you a slap to turn your face?'

In the end I convinced her.

She melted at once. She sat down in the hammock and said, 'Come and sit down by me, son.'

Just then the crazy fit came on me.

I got very angry for no reason at all and I said, 'No, I not going to sit by you.'

She laughed and coaxed.

And the angrier she made me.

Slowly the friendliness died away. It had become a struggle between two wills. I was prepared to drown rather than dishonour myself by obeying.

'I ask you to come and sit down here.'

'I not sitting down.'

'Take off your belt.'

I took it off and gave it to her. She belted me soundly,

and my nose bled, but still I didn't sit in the hammock.

At times like these I used to cry, without meaning it, 'If my father was alive you wouldn't be behaving like this.'

So she remained the enemy. She was someone from whom I was going to escape as soon as I grew big enough. That was, in fact, the main lure of adulthood.

Progress was sweeping through Port-of-Spain in those days. The Americans were pouring money into Trinidad and there was a lot of talk from the British about colonial development and welfare.

One of the visible signs of this progress was the disappearance of the latrines. I hated the latrines, and I used to wonder about the sort of men who came with their lorries at night and carted away the filth; and there was always the horrible fear of falling into a pit.

One of the first men to have decent lavatories built was Hat, and we made a great thing of knocking down his old latrine. All the boys and men went to give a hand. I was too small to give a hand, but I went to watch. The walls were knocked down one by one and in the end there was only one remaining.

Hat said, 'Boys, let we try to knock this one down in one big piece.'

And they did.

The wall swayed and began to fall.

I must have gone mad in that split second, for I did a Superman act and tried to prevent the wall falling.

I just remember people shouting, 'O God! Look out!'

I was travelling in a bus, one of the green buses of Sam's Super Service, from Port-of-Spain to Petit Valley. The bus was full of old women in bright bandanas carrying big baskets of eddoes, yams, bananas, with here and there some chickens. Suddenly the old women all began chattering, and the chickens began squawking. My head felt as though it would split, but when I tried to shout at the old women I found I couldn't open my mouth. I tried again, but all I heard, more distinctly now, was the constant chattering.

Water was pouring down my face.

I was flat out under a tap and there were faces above me looking down.

Somebody shouted, 'He recover. Is all right.'

Hat said, 'How you feeling?'

I said, trying to laugh, 'I feeling all right.'

Mrs Bhakcu said, 'You have any pains?'

I shook my head.

But, suddenly, my whole body began to ache. I tried to move my hand and it hurt.

I said, 'I think I break my hand.'

But I could stand, and they made me walk into the house.

My mother came and I could see her eyes glassy and wet with tears.

Somebody, I cannot remember who, said, 'Boy, you had your mother really worried.'

I looked at her tears, and I felt I was going to cry too. I had discovered that she could be worried and anxious for me.

I wished I were a Hindu god at that moment, with two hundred arms, so that all two hundred could be broken, just to enjoy that moment, and to see again my mother's tears.

1955

Greenie and Yellow

And Bluey is the hero of this story.

At first Bluey belonged to the Welsh couple in the basement. We heard him throughout the house but we hardly saw him. I used to see him only when I went down to the dustbins just outside the basement window. He was smoky blue; lively, almost querulous, with unclipped wings, he made his cage seem too small.

When the Welsh couple had to go back to Wales – I think Mrs Lewis was going to have a baby – they decided to give Bluey to Mrs Cooksey, the landlady. We were surprised when she accepted. She didn't like the Lewises. In fact, she didn't like any of her tenants. She criticized them all to me and I suppose she criticized me to them. You couldn't blame her: the house was just too full of tenants. Apart from a sittingroom on the ground floor, a kitchen on the landing at the top of the basement steps, and a bedroom somewhere in the basement, the whole of the Cookseys' house had been let. The Cookseys had no children and were saving up for old age. It had come but they didn't know.

Mrs Cooksey was delighted with Bluey. She used to lie in wait behind her half-opened door and spring out at us as we passed through the hall; but now it wasn't to ask who had taken more than his share of the milk or who had left the bath dirty; it was to call us into her room to look at Bluey and listen to him, and to admire the improvements she had made to his cage.

The cage, when I had seen it in the basement window, was an elegant little thing with blue bars to match Bluey's feathers, two toy trapezes, a seed-trough, a water-trough and a spring door. Now every Friday there were additions: Mrs Cooksey shopped on Friday. The first addition was toy ferris wheel in multicoloured plastic. The second was a seed-bell; it tinkled when Bluey pecked at it. The third was a small round mirror. Just when it seemed that these additions were going to leave little room for Bluey, Mrs Cooksey added something else. She said it was a friend for Bluey. The friend was a red-beaked chicken emerging from a neatly serrated shell, all in plastic and weighted at the bottom to stay upright.

Bluey loved his toys. He kept the chicken and shell swaying, the trapezes going, the ferris wheel spinning, the seed-bell ringing. He clucked and chattered and whistled and every now and then gave a zestful little shriek.

But he couldn't talk. For that Mrs Cooksey blamed Mrs Lewis. 'They're just like children, d'you see? You've got to train them. But she didn't have the time. Very delicate she was. Just a romp and a giggle all day long.'

Mrs Cooksey bought a booklet, *Your Budgie*, and kept it under the heavy glass ashtray on the table. She said it was full of good hints; and when she had read them, she began to train Bluey. She talked and talked to him, to get him used to her voice. Then she gave him a name: Joey. Bluey never recognized it. When I went down to pay for the milk one Saturday Mrs Cooksey told me that she was also finger-training him, getting him to come out of his cage and remain on her finger. Two or three days later she called me in to get Bluey down from the top of the curtains where he was squawking and shrieking and flapping his wings with energy. He wouldn't come down to calls of 'Joey!' or to Mrs Cooksey's cluckings or to her outstretched finger. I had a lot of trouble before I got him back into his cage.

The finger-training was dropped and the name Joey was dropped. Mrs Cooksey just called him Bluey.

Spring came. The plane tree two back-gardens away, the

only tree between the backs of the houses and the back of
what we were told was the largest cinema in England, became touched with green. The sun shone on some days and
for an hour or two lit up our back-garden, or rather the
Cookseys' garden: tenants weren't allowed. Mrs Cooksey put
Bluey and his cage outside and sat beside him, knitting a bed-
jacket. Sparrows flew about the cage; but they came to dig up
Mr Cooksey's cindery, empty flowerbeds, not to attack
Bluey. And Bluey was aware of no danger. He hopped from
trapeze to trapeze, spun his ferris wheel, rubbed his beak
against his little mirror and cooed at his reflection. His
seed-bell tinkled, the red-beaked chicken bobbed up and
down. Bluey was never to be so happy again.

Coming into the hall late one Friday afternoon I saw that
Mrs Cooksey's door was ajar. I let her take me by surprise.
Behind her pink-rimmed glasses her watery blue eyes were
full of mischief. I followed her into the room.

   Bluey was not alone. He had a companion. A live one. It
was a green budgerigar.

   'He just flew into the garden this morning,' Mrs Cooksey
said. 'Really. Oh, he must have been a smart fellow to get
away from all those naughty little sparrows. Smart, aren't
you, Greenie?'

   Greenie was plumper than Bluey and I thought he had an
arrogant breast. He wasted no time showing us what he
could do. He fanned out one wing with a series of small snap-
ping sounds, folded it back in, and fanned out the other. He
could lean over sideways on one leg too, and when he pecked
at a bar it didn't look so strong. He was noisier than Bluey
and, for all his size, more nimble. He looked the sort of
budgerigar who could elude sparrows. But his experience of
freedom and his triumph over danger had made him something of a bully. Even while we stood over the cage he baited
Bluey. By shrieks and flutterings he attracted Bluey to the
ferris wheel. Bluey went, gave the wheel a spin with his
beak and stood by to give another. Before he could do so,

Greenie flew at him, flapping his wings so powerfully that the sand on the floor of the cage flew up. Bluey retreated, complaining. Greenie outsquawked his complaints. The ferris wheel meant nothing to Greenie; in his wanderings he hadn't picked up the art of making a wheel spin. After some moments he flew away from the wheel and rested on a trapeze. He invited Bluey to the wheel again. Bluey went, and the whole shameful squabble began all over.

Mrs Cooksey was giving little oohs and ahs. 'You have a real friend now, haven't you, Bluey?'

Bluey wasn't listening. He was hurrying away from the wheel to the red-beaked chicken. He pecked at it frenziedly.

'Just like children,' Mrs Cooksey said. 'They'll quarrel and fight, but they are good friends.'

Life became hard for Bluey. Greenie never stopped showing off; and Bluey, continually baited and squawked at, retaliated less and less. At the end of a week he seemed to have lost the will even to protest. It was Greenie now who kept the little trapeze going. Greenie who punched the seed-bell and made it ring, Greenie who filled the room with noise. Mrs Cooksey didn't try to teach Greenie to talk and I don't imagine the thought of finger-training him ever entered her head. 'Greenie's a big boy,' she said.

It gave me some pleasure to see how the big boy fretted at the ferris wheel. He shook it and made it rattle; but he couldn't make it spin.

'Why don't you show him, Bluey?' Mrs Cooksey said.

But Bluey had lost interest in all Mrs Cooksey's embellishments, even in the plastic chicken. He remained on the floor of the cage and hardly moved. Finally he stood quite still, his feathers permanently ruffled, shivering from time to time. His eyes were half-shut and the white lined lids looked tender and vulnerable. His feet began to swell until they became white and scaly.

'He's just hopeless,' Mrs Cooksey said, with surprising vehemence. 'Don't blame Greenie. I did my best to train Bluey. He didn't care. And who's paying for it now?'

She was contrite a few days later. 'It isn't his fault, poor little Bluey. He's got ingrowing toe-nails. And his feet are so dirty too. He hasn't had a bath for a long time.'

I stayed to watch. Mrs Cooksey emptied the glass ashtray of pins and paper-clips and elastic bands and filled it with warm water. She turned on the electric fire and warmed a towel in front of it. She put a hand into the cage, had it pecked and squawked at by Greenie, pulled Bluey out and dropped him into the water in the ashtray. Instantly Bluey dwindled to half his size. His feathers stuck to him like second skin. He was rubbed with carbolic soap, rinsed in the ashtray and dried in the warm towel. At the end he looked damp and dishevelled. 'There you are, Bluey. Dry. And now let's have a look at your little nails.' She put Bluey on the palm of her left hand and held a pair of nail scissors to his swollen feet. A month before, given such freedom, Bluey would have flown to the top of the curtains. Now he lay still. Suddenly he shrieked and gave a little wriggle.

'Poor little Bluey,' Mrs Cooksey said. 'We've cut his little foot.'

Bluey didn't recover. His feet became scalier, more swollen, and gnarled. A paper-thin growth, shaped like a fingernail, appeared on his lower beak and grew upwards, making it hard for him to eat, impossible for him to peck. The top of his beak broke out into a sponge-like sore.

And now even Greenie no longer baited him.

In the summer Mr Cooksey did something he had been talking about for a long time. He painted the hall and the stairs. The paint he used was a dull ordinary blue which quickly revealed extraordinary qualities. It didn't dry. The inside of the door became smudged and dirty and all up the banisters there were streaks of sticky blue from the fingers of tenants. Mr Cooksey painted the door again, adding a notice: WET PAINT PLEASE, with the PLEASE underlined three times. He also chalked warnings on the steps outside. But after a fortnight the paint hadn't dried and it looked as though the door would have to be painted again. Mr Cooksey left notices on the glass-topped table in the hall, each note curter than the last. He had a good command of curt language. This wasn't surprising, because Mr Cooksey was a commissionaire or caretaker or something like that at the head office of an important public corporation. Anyway, it was a big position: he told me he had thirty-four cleaners under him.

I never got used to the wet paint and one day, as I came into the hall, wondering in my exasperation whether I shouldn't wipe the paint off on to the wallpaper, the Cookseys' door opened and I saw Mr Cooksey.

' 'Ave a drink,' he said. 'Cocktail.'

I feared Mr Cooksey's cocktails: they were too obviously one of the perquisites of his calling. But I went in, wiping my fingers on my evening paper. The room smelled of paint and linseed oil.

Mrs Cooksey sat in her armchair and beamed at me. Her hands were resting a little too demurely on her lap. She clearly had something to show.

The cage on the sewing machine was covered with a blue cloth, part of one of Mrs Cooksey's old dresses. It was late evening, still light outside, but dark inside: the Cookseys didn't like to use more electricity than was strictly necessary. Mr Cooksey passed around his cocktails. Mrs Cooksey refused with a shake of the head, I accepted but delayed sipping, Mr Cooksey sipped.

Muted rustlings and tumblings and cheeps came from behind the blue cloth. Mr and Mrs Cooksey sat silent and listened. I listened.

'Got a new one,' Mr Cooksey said, sipping his cocktail and smacking his lips with a little *pop-pop* sound.

'He came into the garden too?' I asked.

'It's a *she!*' Mrs Cooksey cried.

'*Pop-pop*. Ten bob,' said Mr Cooksey. 'Man wanted twelve and six.'

'And we've got a nesting-box for her too.'

'But we didn't pay for that, Bess.'

Mrs Cooksey went and stood by the cage. She rested her hands on the blue cloth, delaying the unveiling. 'She's the daintiest little thing.'

'Yellow,' said Mr Cooksey.

'Just the sort of mate for Greenie.' And, with a flourish, Mrs Cooksey lifted the blue cloth from the cage.

It wasn't the cage I had known. It was a bigger, cruder thing, made from wire netting, with rudimentary embellishments – just two bars supported on the wire netting. And I saw Greenie alone. He had composed himself to sleep. Yellow I didn't see.

Mrs Cooksey giggled, enjoying my disappointment. 'She's there all right. But *in her nesting-box*!' I saw a small wooden box hanging at the back of the cage. Mrs Cooksey tapped it. 'Come out, Yellow. Let Uncle have a look at you. Come out, come out. We know where you are.' Through the round hole of the box a little yellow head popped out, restlessly turning this way and that. Mrs Cooksey tapped the box again, and Yellow slipped out of the box into the cage.

Yellow was smaller than Greenie or Bluey. She wandered about the cage fussily, inquisitively. She certainly had no intention of going to sleep just yet, and she wasn't going to let Greenie sleep either. She hopped up to where he stood on his bar, his head hunched into his breast, and pecked at him. Greenie shook himself but didn't open his eyes. Yellow gave him a push. Perhaps it was chivalry – though I had never credited Greenie with that – or perhaps he was just too sleepy. But Greenie didn't fight back. He yielded and yielded until he could move no further. Then he went down to the other bar. Yellow followed. When she had dislodged him a second time she lost interest in him and went back into her nesting-box.

'D'you see?' Mrs Cooksey said. 'She's interested. The man at the shop says that when they're interested you can expect eggs in ten days.'

'Twelve, Bess.'

'He told *me* ten.'

I tried to get them off the subject. I said, 'They've got a new cage.'

'Mr Cooksey made it.'

Mr Cooksey pop-popped.

He had painted it too. With the blue paint.

Yellow pushed her head through the hole of her box.

'Oh, she *is* interested.' Mrs Cooksey replaced the blue cloth on the cage. 'We mustn't be naughty. Leave them alone.'

'One of my cleaners,' Mr Cooksey said, pausing and throwing the possessive adjective into relief, 'one of my cleaners keeps chickens and turkeys. Makes a packet at Christmas. Nabsolute packet.'

Mrs Cooksey said, 'I wouldn't like to sell any of my little Greenies and Yellows.'

Abruptly I remembered. 'Where's Bluey?'

I don't think Mrs Cooksey liked being reminded. She showed me where Bluey's cage was, on the floor, over-shadowed by an armchair and the bookcase that had few books and many china animals. Alone among the luxurious furnishings of his cage, Bluey stood still, on one foot, his feathers ruffled, his head sunk low.

'I can't throw him out, can I?' Mrs Cooksey shrugged her shoulders. 'I've done my best for him.'

The love life didn't agree with Greenie.

'She's taming him,' Mrs Cooksey said.

He had certainly quietened down.

'P'raps he's missing Bluey,' Mr Cooksey said.

'Hark at him,' said Mrs Cooksey.

Yellow was still eager, restless, inquisitive, going in and out of her box. Mrs Cooksey showed me how cleverly the box had been made: you could slide out the back to see if there were eggs. She counted the days.

'Seven days now.'

'Nine, Bess.'

'Seven.'

Then: 'Greenie's playing the fool,' Mr Cooksey said.

'Look who's talking,' Mrs Cooksey said.

Two days later she met me in the hall and said, 'Something's happened to Greenie.'

I went to look. Greenie had the same unhealthy stillness as Bluey now: his feathers were ruffled, his eyes half-closed, his head sunk into his breast. Yellow fussed about him, not belligerently or playfully, but in puzzlement.

'She *loves* him, d'you see? I've tried to feed him. Milk from an eye-dropper. But he isn't taking a thing. Tell me where it hurts, Greenie. Tell Mummy where.'

It was Friday. When Mrs Cooksey rang up the RSPCA they told her to bring Greenie in on Monday. All during the week-end Greenie deteriorated. Mrs Cooksey did her best. Although it was warm she kept the electric fire going all the time, a luxury the Cookseys denied themselves even in winter. A towel was always warming in front of the fire. Greenie was wrapped in another towel.

On Monday Mrs Cooksey wrapped Greenie in a clean towel and took him to the doctor. He prescribed a fluid of some sort and warned Mrs Cooksey against giving Greenie milk.

'He said something about poison,' Mrs Cooksey said. 'As though I would want to do anything to my Greenie. But you should have seen the doctor. Doctor! He was just a boy. He told me to bring Greenie again on Friday. That's four days.'

When I came in next evening, my fingers stained with blue paint from the door, Mrs Cooksey met me in the hall. I followed her into the room.

'Greenie's dead,' she said. She was very calm.

The door opened authoritatively and Mr Cooksey came in, mackintoshed and bowler-hatted.

'Greenie's dead,' Mrs Cooksey said.

'*Pop-pop.*' Mr Cooksey took off his hat and mackintosh and rested them carefully on the chair next to the sideboard.

In the silence that followed I didn't look at the Cookseys or at the cage on the sewing machine. It was dark in the corner where Bluey's cage was and it was some moments before I could see things clearly. Bluey's cage was empty. I looked up at the sewing machine. He was in the cage with Yellow; he drooped on the floor, eyes closed, one swollen foot raised. Yellow paid him no attention. She fussed about from bar to bar, with a faint continuous rustle. Then she slipped through the hole into the nesting-box and was silent.

'She's still *interested*,' Mr Cooksey said. He looked at Bluey. 'You never know.'

'It's no good,' Mrs Cooksey said. 'She loved Greenie.' Her old woman's face had broken up and she was crying.

Mr Cooksey opened doors on the sideboard, noisily looking for cocktails.

Mrs Cooksey blew her nose. 'Oh, they're like children. You get so fond of them.'

It was hard to think of something to say. I said, 'We were all fond of Greenie, Mrs Cooksey. I was fond of him and I am sure Mr Cooksey was too.'

'*Pop-pop.*'

'Him? He doesn't care. He's *tough*. D'you know, he had a look at Greenie this morning. Told me he looked better. But he's always like that. Look at him. Nothing worries him.'

'Not true, Bess. Was a trific shock. Trific.'

Yellow never came out of her nesting-box. She died two days later and Mrs Cooksey buried her in the garden, next to Greenie. I saw the cage and the nesting-box, smashed, on the heap of old wood Mr Cooksey kept in the garden shed.

In the Cookseys' sittingroom Bluey and his cage took their place again on the sewing machine. Slowly, week by week, Bluey improved. The time came when he could stand on both feet, when he could shuffle an inch or two on the floor of his cage. But his feet were never completely well

again, and the growths on his beak didn't disappear. The
trapezes never swung and the ferris wheel was still.

It must have been three months later. I went down one
Saturday morning to pay Mrs Cooksey for the milk. I had to
get some change and she had to hunt about for her glasses,
then for the vase in which she kept small change. She poured
out buttons from one vase, pins from another, fasteners from
a third.

'Poor old lady,' she kept on muttering – that was how she
had taken to speaking of herself. She fumbled about with
more cases, then stopped, twisted her face into a smile and
held out her open palm towards me. On it I saw two latch
keys and a small white skull, finished, fragile.

'Greenie or Yellow,' she said. 'I couldn't really tell you
which. The sparrows dug it up.'

We both looked at Bluey in his cage.

1957

The Perfect Tenants

We heard about the Dakins before they arrived. 'They're the perfect tenants,' Mrs Cooksey, the landlady, said. 'Their landlady brought them to me personally. She says she's sorry to lose them, but she's leaving London and taking over a hotel in Benson.'

The Dakins moved in so quietly it was some days before I realized they were in the house. On Saturday and Sunday I heard sounds of washing and scrubbing and carpet-sweeping from the flat above. On Monday there was silence again.

Once or twice that week I saw them on the steps. Mrs Dakin was about forty, tall and thin, with a sweet smile. 'She used to be a policewoman,' Mrs Cooksey said. 'Sergeant, I think.' Mr Dakin was as old as his wife and looked as athletic. But his rough, handsome face was humourless. His greetings were brief and firm and didn't encourage conversation.

Their behaviour was exemplary. They never had visitors. They never had telephone calls. Their cooking never smelled. They never allowed their milk bottles to accumulate and at the same time they never left an empty milk bottle on the doorstep in daylight. And they were silent. They had no radio. The only sounds were of scrubbing brush, broom and carpet-sweeper. Sometimes at night, when the street fell silent, I heard them in their bedroom: a low whine punctuated infrequently with brief bass rumbles.

'There's respectable people in every class,' Mrs Cooksey said. 'The trouble these days is that you never know where you are. Look at the Seymours. Creeping up late at night to the bathroom and splashing about together. You can't even trust the BBC people. Remember that Arab.'

The Dakins quickly became the favourite tenants. Mr Cooksey invited Mr Dakin down to 'cocktails'. Mrs Dakin had Mrs Cooksey up to tea and Mrs Cooksey told us that she was satisfied with the appearance of the flat. 'They're very fussy,' Mrs Cooksey said. She knew no higher praise, and we all felt reproached.

It was from Mrs Cooksey that I learned with disappointment that the Dakins had their troubles. 'He fell off a ladder and broke his arm, but they won't pay any compensation. The arm's bent and he can't even go to the seaside. What's more, he can't do his job properly. He's an electrician, and you know how they're always climbing. But there you are, d'you see. *They* don't care. What's three hundred pounds to *them*? But will they give it? Do you know the foreman actually burned the ladder?'

I hadn't noticed any disfigurement about Mr Dakin. He had struck me as a man of forbidding vigour, but now I looked on him with greater interest and respect for putting up so silently with misfortune. We often passed on the stairs but never did more than exchange greetings, and so it might have gone on had it not been for the Cookseys' New Year's Eve party.

At that time I was out of favour with the Cookseys. I had left a hoard of about fifteen milk bottles on the doorstep and the milkman had refused to take them all at once. For a whole day six partly washed milk bottles had remained on the doorstep, lowering Mrs Cooksey's house. Some unpleasantness between Mrs Cooksey and the milkman had followed and quickly been passed on to me.

When I came in that evening the door of the Cookseys' sittingroom was open and through it came laughter, stamping and television music. Mr Cooksey, coming from the kitchen with a tray, looked at me in embarrassment. He brought his lips rapidly over his false teeth and made a popping sound.

'*Pop-pop*. Come in,' he said. 'Drink. Cocktail.'

I went in. Mrs Cooksey was sober but gay. The laughter and the stamping came from the Dakins alone. They were dancing. Mrs Dakin shrieked whenever Mr Dakin spun her around, and for a man whose left arm was permanently damaged he was doing it quite well. When she saw me Mrs Dakin shrieked, and Mrs Cooksey giggled, as though it was her duty to cheer the Dakins up. The couple from the flat below mine were there too, she on the seat of an armchair, he on the arm. They were dressed in their usual sub-county manner and looked constrained and unhappy. I thought of this couple as the Knitmaster and the Knitmistress. They had innumerable minor possessions: contemporary coffee tables and lampstands, a Cona coffee machine, a record-player, a portable television-and-VHF set, a 1946 Anglia which at the appropriate season carried a sticker: FREE LIFT TO GLYNDEBOURNE AT YOUR OWN RISK, and a Knitmaster machine which was never idle for long.

The music stopped, Mrs Dakin pretended to swoon into her husband's injured arms, and Mrs Cooksey clapped.

' 'Elp yourself, 'elp yourself,' Mr Cooksey shouted.

'Another drink, darling?' the Knitmaster whispered to his wife.

'Yes, yes,' Mrs Dakin cried.

The Knitmistress smiled malevolently at Mrs Dakin.

'Whisky?' said Mr Cooksey. 'Beer? Sherry? Guinness?'

'Give her the cocktail,' Mrs Cooksey said.

Mr Cooksey's cocktails were well known to his older tenants. He had a responsible position in an important public corporation – he said he had thirty-four cleaners under him – and the origin and blend of his cocktails were suspect.

The Knitmistress took the cocktail and sipped without enthusiasm.

'And you?' Mr Cooksey asked.

'Guinness,' I said.

'Guinness!' Mr Dakin exclaimed, looking at me for the first time with interest and kindliness. 'Where did you learn to drink Guinness?'

We drew closer and talked about Guinness.

'Of course it's best in Ireland,' he said. 'Thick and creamy. What's it like where you come from?'

'I can't drink it there. It's too warm.'

Mr Dakin shook his head. 'It isn't the climate. It's the Guinness. It can't travel. It gets sick.'

Soon it was time to sing Auld Lang Syne.

The next day the Dakins reverted to their exemplary behaviour, but now when we met we stopped to have a word about the weather.

One evening, about four weeks later, I heard something like a commotion in the flat above. Footsteps pounded down the stairs, there was a banging on my door, and Mrs Dakin rushed in and cried, 'It's my 'usband! 'E's rollin' in agony.'

Before I could say anything she ran out and raced down to the Knitmasters.

'My husband's rollin' in agony.'

The whirring of the Knitmaster machine stopped and I heard the Knitmistress making sympathetic sounds.

The Knitmaster said, 'Telephone for the doctor.'

I went and stood on the landing as a sympathetic gesture. Mrs Dakin roused the Cookseys, there were more exclamations, then I heard the telephone being dialled. I went back to my room. After some thought I left my door wide open: another gesture of sympathy.

Mrs Dakin, Mrs Cooksey and Mr Cooksey hurried up the stairs.

The Knitmaster machine was whirring again.

Presently there was a knock on my door and Mr Cooksey came in. '*Pop-pop*. It's as hot as a bloomin' oven up there.' He puffed out his cheeks. 'No wonder he's ill.'

I asked after Mr Dakin.

'A touch of indigestion, if you ask me.' Then, like a man

used to more momentous events, he added, 'One of my cleaners took ill sudden last week. Brain tumour.'

The doctor came and the Dakins' flat was full of footsteps and conversation. Mr Cooksey ran up and down the steps, panting and pop-popping. Mrs Dakin was sobbing and Mrs Cooksey was comforting her. An ambulance bell rang in the street and soon Mr Dakin, Mrs Dakin and the doctor left.

'Appendix,' Mr Cooksey told me.

The Knitmaster opened his door.

'Appendix,' Mr Cooksey shouted down. 'It was like an oven up there.'

'He was cold,' Mrs Cooksey said.

'Pah!'

Mrs Cooksey looked anxious.

'Nothing to it, Bess,' Mr Cooksey said. ' 'Itler had the appendix took out of all his soldiers.'

The Knitmaster said, 'I had mine out two years ago. Small scar.' He measured off the top of his forefinger. 'About that long. It's a nervous thing really. You get it when you are depressed or worried. My wife had to have hers out just before we went to France.'

The Knitmistress came out and smiled her terrible smile, baring short square teeth and tall gums, and screwing up her small eyes. She said, 'Hullo,' and pulled on woollen gloves, which perhaps she had just knitted on her machine. She wore a tweed skirt, a red sweater, a brown velveteen jacket and a red-and-white beret.

'Appendix,' Mr Cooksey said.

The Knitmistress only smiled again, and followed her husband downstairs to the 1946 Anglia.

'A terrible thing,' I said to Mrs Cooksey tentatively.

'*Pop-pop.*' Mr Cooksey looked at his wife.

'Terrible thing,' Mrs. Cooksey said.

Our quarrel over the milk bottles was over.

Mr Cooksey became animated. 'Nothing to it, Bess. Just a lot of fuss for nothing at all. Gosh, they kept that room like an oven.'

Mrs Dakin came back at about eleven. Her eyes were red but she was composed. She spoke about the kindness of the nurses. And then, to round off an unusual evening, I heard – at midnight on a weekday – the sound of the carpet-sweeper upstairs. The Knitmistress complained in her usual way. She opened her door and talked loudly to her husband about the nuisance.

Next morning Mrs Dakin went again to the hospital. She returned just before midday and as soon as she got into the hall she began to sob so loudly that I heard her on the second floor.

I found her in Mrs Cooksey's arms when I went down. Mrs Cooksey was pale and her eyes were moist.

'What's happened?' I whispered.

Mrs Cooksey shook her head.

Mrs Dakin leaned against Mrs Cooksey, who was much smaller.

'And my brother is getting married tomorrow!' Mrs Dakin burst out.

'Come now, Eva,' Mrs Cooksey said firmly. 'Tell me what happened at the hospital.'

'They're feeding him through a glass tube. They've put him on the danger list. And – his bed is near the door!'

'That doesn't mean anything, Eva.'

'It does! It does!'

'Nonsense, Eva.'

'They've got him screened round.'

'You must be brave, Eva.'

We led Mrs Dakin to Mrs Cooksey's sittingroom, made her sit down and watched her cry.

'It burst inside 'im.' Mrs Dakin made a wild gesture across her body. 'They had to cut him clean open, and – *scrape* it out.' Having uttered this terrible word, she abandoned herself to her despair.

'Come now, Eva,' Mrs Cooksey said. 'He wouldn't like you to behave like this.'

We all took turns to look after Mrs Dakin between her trips to the hospital. The news didn't get better. Mrs Dakin had tea with the Cookseys. She had tea with the Knitmistress. She had tea with me. We talked gaily about everything except the sick man, and Mrs Dakin was very brave. She even related some of her adventures in the police force. She also complained.

'The first thing Mr Cooksey said when he came up that evening was that the room was like an oven. But I couldn't help that. My husband was cold. Fancy coming up and saying a thing like that!'

I gave Mrs Dakin many of the magazines which had been piling up on the enormous Victorian dresser in my kitchen. The Knitmistress, I noticed, was doing the same thing.

Mr Cooksey allowed himself to grow a little grave. He discussed the operation in a sad but clinical way. 'When it bursts inside 'em, you see, it poisons the whole system. That's why they had to cut 'im open. Clean it out. They hardly ever live afterwards.'

Mrs Cooksey said, 'He was such a nice man. I am so glad now we enjoyed ourselves on New Year's Eve. It's her I'm really sorry for. He was her second, you know.'

'Aah,' Mr Cooksey said. 'There are women like that.'

I told the Knitmistress, 'And he was such a nice man.'

'Wasn't he?'

I heard Mrs Dakin sobbing in everybody's rooms. I heard her sobbing on the staircase.

Mrs Cooksey said, 'It's all so terrible. Her brother got married yesterday, but she couldn't go to the wedding. She had to send a telegram. They are coming up to see Mr Dakin. What a thing to happen on anybody's honeymoon!'

Mrs Dakin's brother and his bride came up from Wales on a motorbike. Mrs Dakin was at the hospital when they came and Mrs Cooksey gave them tea.

I didn't see Mrs Dakin that evening, but late that night I saw the honeymoon couple running upstairs with bottles wrapped in tissue paper. He was a huge man – a footballer, Mrs Cooksey said – and when he ran up the steps you heard it all over the house. His bride was small, countrified and gay. They stayed awake for some time.

Next morning, when I went down to get the paper, I saw the footballer's motorbike on the doorstep. It had leaked a lot of oil.

Again that day Mrs Dakin didn't come to our rooms. And that evening there was another party in the flat above. We heard the footballer's heavy footsteps, his shouts, his wife's giggles, Mrs Dakin's whine.

Mrs Dakin had ceased to need our solace. It was left to us to ask how Mr Dakin was getting on, whether he had liked the magazines we had sent, whether he wanted any more. Then, as though reminded of some sadness bravely forgotten, Mrs Dakin would say yes, Mr Dakin thanked us.

Mrs Cooksey didn't like the new reticence. Nor did the rest of us. For some time, though, the Knitmaster persevered and he had his reward when two days later Mrs Dakin said, 'I told 'im what you said about the nervousness, and he wondered how you ever knew.' And she repeated the story about the fall from the defective ladder, the bent arm, the foreman burning the ladder.

We were astonished. It was our first indication that the Dakins were taking an interest in the world outside the hospital.

'Well, really!' Mrs Cooksey said.

The Knitmistress began to complain about the noise in the evenings.

'Pah!' Mr Cooksey said. 'It *couldn't* 'ave burst inside him. Feeding through a glass tube!'

We heard the honeymoon couple bounding down the stairs. The front door slammed, then we heard the thunderous stutter of the motorbike.

'He could be had up,' Mr Cooksey said. 'No silencer.'

'Well!' Mrs Cooksey said. 'I am glad *somebody's* having a nice time. So cheap too. Where do you think they're off to?'

'Not the hospital,' Mr Cooksey said. 'Football, more likely.'

This reminded him. The curtains were drawn, the tiny television set turned on. We watched horse-racing, then part of the football match. Mrs Cooksey gave me tea. Mr Cooksey offered me a cigarette. I was back in favour.

The next day, eight days after Mr Dakin had gone to the hospital, I met Mrs Dakin outside the tobacconist's. She was shopping and her bulging bag reflected the gaiety on her face.

'He's coming back tomorrow,' she said.

I hadn't expected such a rapid recovery.

'Everybody at the hospital was surprised,' Mrs Dakin said. 'But it's because he's so strong, you see.' She opened her shopping bag. 'I've got some sherry and whisky and' – she laughed – 'some Guinness of course. And I'm buying a duck, to have with apple sauce. He loves apple sauce. He says the apple sauce helps the duck to go down.'

I smiled at the little family joke. Then Mrs Dakin asked me, 'Guess who went to the hospital yesterday.'

'Your brother and his wife.'

She shook her head. 'The foreman!'

'The one who burned the ladder?'

'Oh, and he was ever so nice. He brought grapes and magazines and told my husband he wasn't to worry about anything. They're frightened now all right. As soon as my husband went to hospital my solicitor wrote them a letter. And my solicitor says we stand a good chance of getting more than three hundred pounds now.'

I saw the Knitmaster on the landing that evening and told him about Mr Dakin's recovery.

'Complications couldn't have been serious,' he said. 'But it's a nervous thing. A nervous thing.'

The Knitmistress opened the kitchen door.

'He's coming back tomorrow,' the Knitmaster said.

The Knitmistress gave me one of her terrible smiles.

'Five hundred pounds for falling off a ladder,' Mr Cooksey said. 'Ha! It's as easy as falling off a log, ain't it, Bess?'

Mrs Cooksey sighed. 'That's what the Labour has done to this country. They didn't do a thing for the middle class.'

'Bent arm! Can't go to the seaside! Pamperin', that's what it is. You wouldn't've found 'Itler pampering that lot.'

A motorbike lacerated the silence.

'Our happy honeymooners,' Mr Cooksey said.

'They'll soon be leaving,' Mrs Cooksey said, and went out to meet them in the hall.

'Whose key are you using?'

'Eva's,' the footballer said, running up the stairs.

'We'll see about that,' Mrs Cooksey called.

Mrs Dakin said: 'I went down to Mrs Cooksey and I said, "Mrs Cooksey, what do you mean by insulting my guests? It's bad enough for them having their honeymoon spoilt without being insulted." And she said she'd let the flat to me and my 'usband and not to my brother and his wife and they'd have to go. And I told her that they were leaving to-morrow anyway because my husband's coming back to-morrow. And I told her I hoped she was satisfied that she'd spoiled their honeymoon, which comes only once in a life-time. And she said some people managed to have two, which I took as a reference to myself because, as you know, my first husband died during the war. And then I told her that if that was the way she was going to behave then I could have nothing more to say to her. And she said she hoped I would have the oil from my brother's bike cleaned up. And I said that if it wasn't for my husband being so ill I would've given notice then and there. And she said it was *because* my husband was ill that she didn't give me notice, which any other land-lady would've done.'

Three things happened the next day. The footballer and his wife left. Mrs Dakin told me that the firm had given her husband four hundred pounds. And Mr Dakin returned from hospital, no more noticed by the rest of the house than if he had returned from a day's work. No sounds came from the Dakins' flat that evening except for the whine and rumble of conversation.

Two days later I heard Mrs Dakin racing down to my flat. She knocked and entered at the same time. 'The telly's coming today,' she said.

Mr Dakin was going to put up the aerial himself. I wondered whether he was as yet strong enough to go climbing about the roof.

'They wanted ten pounds to do it. But my husband's an electrician and he can do it himself. You must come up tonight. We're going to celebrate.'

I went up. A chromium-plated aeroplane and a white doily had been placed on the television set. It looked startlingly new.

Mrs Dakin emptied a bottle of Tio Pepe into three tumblers.

'To good 'ealth,' she said, and we drank to that.

Mr Dakin looked thin and fatigued. But his fatigue was tinged with a certain quiet contentment. We watched a play about a 400-year-old man who took certain drugs and looked no more than twenty. From time to time Mrs Dakin gave little cries of pleasure, at the play, the television set, and the quality of the sherry.

Mr Dakin languidly took up the empty bottle and studied the label. '*Spanish* sherry,' he said.

Mr Cooksey waylaid me the following day. 'Big telly they've got.'

'Eighteen inch.'

'Those big ones hurt the eyes, don't you find?'

'They do.'

'Come in and have a drink. BBC and Commercial?'

I nodded.

'Never did hold with those commercials. Ruining the country. We're not going to have ours adapted.'

'We're waiting for the colour,' Mrs Cooksey said.

Mrs Cooksey loved a battle. She lived for her house alone. She had no relations or friends, and little happened to her or her husband. Once, shortly after Hess had landed in Scotland, Mr Cooksey had been mistaken by a hostile crowd at Victoria Station for Mussolini, but for the most part Mrs Cooksey's conversation was about her victories over tenants. In her battles with them she stuck to the rules. *The Law of Landlord and Tenant* was one of the few books among the many china animals in the large bookcase in her sitting-room. And Mrs Cooksey had her own idea of victory. She never gave anyone notice. That was almost an admission of defeat. Mrs Cooksey asked me, 'You didn't throw a loaf of stale bread into the garden, did you?'

I said I hadn't.

'I didn't think you had. That's what the other people in this street do, you know. It's a fight to keep this house the way it is, I can tell you. There's the mice, d'you see. You haven't any mice up here, have you?'

'As a matter of fact I had one yesterday.'

'I knew it. The moment you let up these things start happening. All the other houses in this street have mice. That's what the sanitary inspector told me. He said this was the cleanest house in the whole street. But the moment you start throwing food about you're bound to get mice.'

That evening I heard Mrs Dakin complaining loudly. She was doing it the way the Knitmistress did: talking loudly to her husband through an open door.

'Coming up here and asking if I had thrown a loaf of bread into 'er 'orrible little garden. And talking about people having too much to eat these days. Well, if it's one thing I like, it is a warm room. I don't wrap myself up in a blanket and *'uddle* in front of cinders and then come and say that somebody else's room is like an oven.'

Mrs Dakin left her kitchen door open and did the washing-up with many bangs, jangles and clatters. The television sound was turned up and in my room I could hear every commercial, every song, every scrap of dialogue. The carpet-sweeper was brought into action; I heard it banging against walls and furniture.

The next day Mrs Cooksey continued her mice hunt. She went into all the flats and took up the linoleum and put wads of newspaper in the gaps between the floorboards. She also emptied Mrs Dakin's dustbin. 'To keep away the mice,' she told us.

I heard the Dakins' television again that night.

The next morning there was a large notice in the hall. I recognized Mr Cooksey's handwriting and style: WILL THE PERSON OR PERSONS RESPONSIBLE SEE ABOUT THE IMMEDIATE REMOVAL OF THE OIL STAINS ON THE FRONT STEPS. In the bathroom there was a notice tied to the pipe that led to the geyser: WILL THE PERSON OR PERSONS WHO HAVE BEEN TAMPERING WITH THIS TAP PLEASE STOP IT. And in the lavatory: WE NEVER THOUGHT WE WOULD HAVE TO MAKE THIS REQUEST BUT WILL THE PERSON OR PERSONS RESPONSIBLE PLEASE LEAVE THESE OFFICES AS THEY WOULD LIKE TO FIND THEM.

The Dakins retaliated at once. Four unwashed milk bottles were placed on the stains on the steps. An empty whisky bottle was placed, label outwards, next to the dustbin.

I felt the Dakins had won that round.

'Liquor and football pools,' Mr Cooksey said. 'That's all that class spends its money on. Pamperin'! You mustn't upset yourself, Bess. We're giving them enough rope to hang themselves.'

The television boomed through the house that evening. The washing-up was done noisily, the carpet-sweeper banged against walls and furniture, and Mrs Dakin sang loudly. Presently I heard scuffling sounds and shrieks. The Dakins were dancing. This went on for a short time. Then I heard a bath being run.

There was a soft knock on my door and Mrs Cooksey came in. 'I just wanted to find out who was having the bath,' she said.

For some moments after she left the bath continued to

run. Then there was a sharper sound of running water, hissing and metallic. And soon the bath was silent.

There was no cistern to feed the geyser ('Unhygienic things, cisterns,' Mr Cooksey said) and the flow of water to it depended on the taps in the house. By turning on a tap in your kitchen you could lessen the flow and the heat of the water from the geyser. The hissing sound indicated that a tap had been turned full on downstairs, rendering the geyser futile.

From the silent bathroom I heard occasional splashes. The hissing sound continued. Then Mr Dakin sneezed.

The bathroom door opened and was closed with a bang. Mr Dakin sneezed again and Mrs Dakin said, 'If you catch pneumonia, I know who your solicitor will have to be writing to next.'

And all they could do was to smash the gas mantle in the bathroom.

It seemed that they had accepted defeat, for they did nothing further the next day. I was with the Cookseys when the Dakins came in from work that afternoon. In a few minutes they had left the house again. The light in the Cookseys' sittingroom had not been turned on and we stared at them through the lace curtains. They walked arm in arm.

'Going to look for a new place, I suppose,' Mr Cooksey said.

There was a knock and the Knitmistress came in, her smile brilliant and terrible even in the gloom. She said, 'Hullo.' Then she addressed Mrs Cooksey: 'Our lights have gone.'

'Power failure,' Mr Cooksey said. But the street lights were on. The light in the Cookseys' room was turned on but nothing happened.

Mrs Cooksey's face fell.

'Fuse,' Mr Cooksey said briskly. He regarded himself as an electrical expert. With the help of a candle he selected fuse wire, went down to the fuse box, urged us to turn off all lights and fires and stoves, and set to work. The wire fused again. And again.

'He's been *up* to something,' Mr Cooksey said.

But we couldn't find out what that was. The Dakins had secured their rooms with new Yale locks.

The Knitmistress complained.

'It's no use, Bess,' Mr Cooksey said. 'You'll just have to give them notice. Never *did* hold with that class of people anyway.'

And defeat was made even more bitter because it turned out that victory had been very close. After Mrs Cooksey asked them to leave, the Dakins announced that they had used part of the compensation money to pay down on a house and were just about to give notice themselves. They packed and left without saying goodbye.

Three weeks later the Dakins' flat was taken over by a middle-aged lady with a fat shining dachshund called Nicky. Her letters were posted on from a ladies' club whose terrifying interiors I had often glimpsed from the top of a number sixteen bus.

1957

The Heart

When they decided that the only way to teach Hari to swim would be to throw him into the sea, Hari dropped out of the sea scouts. Every Monday afternoon for a term he had put on the uniform, practised rowing on the school grounds, and learned to run up signals and make knots. The term before he had dropped out of the boy scouts, to avoid going to camp. At the school sports the term before that he had entered for all the races for the under-elevens, but when the time came he was too shy to strip (the emblem of his house had been fancifully embroidered on his vest by his mother), and he didn't run.

Hari was an only child. He was ten and had a weak heart. The doctors had advised against over-exertion and excitement, and Hari was unexercised and fat. He would have liked to play cricket, fancying himself as a fast bowler, but he was never picked for any of the form teams. He couldn't run quickly, he couldn't bowl, he couldn't bat, and he threw like a girl. He would also have liked to whistle, but he could only make hissing noises through his small plump lips. He had an almost Chinese passion for neatness. He wrote with a blotter below his hand and blotted each line as he wrote; he crossed out with the help of a ruler. His books were clean and unmarked, except on the fly-leaf, where his name had been written by his father. He would have passed unnoticed at school if he hadn't been so well provided with money. This made him unpopular and attracted bullies. His expensive fountain pens were always stolen; and he had learned to stay away from the tuck shop.

Most of the boys from Hari's district who went to the school used Jameson Street. Hari wished to avoid this street. The only way he could do this was to go down Rupert Street. And at the bottom of that street, just where he turned right, there was the house with the Alsatians.

The house stood on the right-hand corner and walking on the other side would have made his cowardice plain, to dogs and passers-by. The Alsatians bounded down from the veranda, barking, leapt against the wire fence and made it shake. Their paws touched the top of the fence and it always seemed to Hari that with a little effort they could jump right over. Sometimes a thin old lady with glasses and grey hair and an irritable expression limped out to the veranda and called in a squeaky voice to the Alsatians. At once they stopped barking, forgot Hari, ran up to the veranda and wagged their heavy tails, as though apologizing for the noise and at the same time asking to be congratulated. The old lady tapped them on the head and they continued to wag their tails; if she slapped them hard they moved away with their heads bowed, their tails between their legs, and lay down on the veranda, gazing out, blinking, their muzzles beneath their forelegs.

Hari envied the old lady her power over the dogs. He was glad when she came out; but he also felt ashamed of his own fear and weakness.

The city was full of unlicensed mongrels who barked in relay all through the day and night. Of these dogs Hari was not afraid. They were thin and starved and cowardly. To drive them away one had only to bend down as though reaching for a stone; it was a gesture the street dogs all understood. But it didn't work with the Alsatians; it merely aggravated their fury.

Four times a day – he went home for lunch – Hari had to pass the Alsatians, hear their bark and breath, see their long white teeth, black lips and red tongues, see their eager, powerful bodies, taller than he when they leapt against the fence. He took his revenge on the street dogs. He picked up imaginary stones; and the street dogs always bolted.

When Hari asked for a bicycle he didn't mention the boys in Jameson Street or the Alsatians in Rupert Street. He spoke about the sun and his fatigue. His parents had misgivings about the bicycle, but Hari learned to ride without accident. And then, with the power of his bicycle, he was no longer afraid of the dogs in Rupert Street. The Alsatians seldom barked at passing cyclists. So Hari stopped in front of the house at the corner, and when the Alsatians ran down from the veranda he pretended to throw things at them until they were thoroughly enraged and their breath grew loud. Then he cycled slowly away, the Alsatians following along the fence to the end of the lot, growling with anger and frustration. Once, when the old lady came out, Hari pretended he had stopped only to tie his laces.

Hari's school was in a quiet, open part of the city. The streets were wide and there were no pavements, only broad, well-kept grass verges. The verges were not level; every few yards there were shallow trenches which drained off the water from the road. Hari liked cycling on the verges, gently rising and falling.

Late one Friday afternoon Hari was cycling back from school after a meeting of the Stamp Club (he had joined that after leaving the sea scouts and with the large collections and expensive albums given him by his father he enjoyed a continuing esteem). It was growing dark as Hari cycled along the verge, falling and rising, looking down at the grass.

In a trench he saw the body of an Alsatian.

The bicycle rolled down into the trench and over the thick tail of the dog. The dog rose and, without looking at Hari, shook himself. Then Hari saw another Alsatian. And another. Steering to avoid them, he ran into more. They lay in the trenches and all over the verge. They were of varying colours; one was brown-black. Hari had not pedalled since he had seen the first dog and was now going so slowly he felt he was losing his balance. From behind him came a low, brief

bark, like a sneeze. At this, energy returned to him. He rode
on to the asphalt and it was only then, as though they too
had just recovered from their surprise, that the Alsatians
all rose and came after him. He pedalled, staring ahead, not
looking at what was behind him or beside him. Three Alsatians, the brown-black one among them, were running
abreast of his bicycle. Calmly, as he pedalled, Hari waited
for their attack. But they only ran beside him, not barking.
The bicycle hummed; the dogs' paws on the asphalt sounded
like pigeons' feet on a tin roof. And then Hari felt that the
savagery of the Alsatians was casual, without anger or
malice: an evening gathering, an evening's pleasure. He
fixed his eyes on the main road at the end, with the street
lamps just going on, the lighted trolley-buses, the motor-
cars, the people.

Then he was there. The Alsatians had dropped behind.
He didn't look for them. It was only when he was in the
main road, with the trolley-poles sparking blue in the night
already fallen, that he realized how frightened he had been,
how close to painful death from the teeth of those happy
dogs. His heart beat fast, from the exertion. Then he felt
a sharp pain he had never known before. He gave a choked,
deep groan and fell off the bicycle.

He spent a month in a nursing home and didn't go to school
for the rest of that term. But he was well enough again when
the new term began. It was decided that he should give up
the bicycle; and his father changed his hours of work so that
he could drive Hari to and from the school.

His birthday fell early that term, and when he was driven
home from school in the afternoon his mother handed him a
basket and said, 'Happy birthday!'

It was a puppy.

'He won't bite you,' his mother said. 'Touch him and
see.'

'Let me see you touch him,' Hari said.

'You must touch him,' his mother said. 'He is yours.

You must get him used to you. They are one-man dogs.'

He thought of the old lady with the squeaky voice and he held out his hand to the puppy. The puppy licked it and pressed a damp nose against it. Hari was tickled. He burst out laughing, felt the puppy's hair and the puppy rubbed against his hand; he passed his hand over the puppy's muzzle, then he lifted the puppy and the puppy licked his face and Hari was tickled into fresh laughter.

The puppy had small sharp teeth and liked to pretend that he was biting. Hari liked the feel of his teeth; there was friendliness in them, and soon there would be power. His power. 'They are one-man dogs,' his mother said.

He got his father to drive to school down Rupert Street. Sometimes he saw the Alsatians. Then he thought of his own dog, and felt protected and revenged. They drove up and down the street with grass verges along which he had been chased by the Alsatians. But he never again saw any Alsatian there.

The puppy was always waiting when they got back home. His father drove right up to the gate and blew his horn. His mother came out to open the gate, and the puppy came out too, wagging his tail, leaping up against the car even as it moved.

'Hold him! Hold him!' Hari cried.

More than anything now he feared losing his dog.

He liked hearing his mother tell visitors about his love for the puppy. And he was given many books about dogs. He learned with sadness that they lived for only twelve years; so that when he was twenty-three, a man, he would have no dog. In the circumstances training seemed pointless, but the books all recommended training, and Hari tried it. The puppy responded with a languor Hari thought enchanting. At school he was moved almost to tears when they read the poem beginning 'A barking sound the shepherd hears'. He went to see the film *Lassie Come Home* and wept. From the film he realized that he had forgotten an important part of the puppy's training. And, to prevent his puppy eating food given by strangers, he dipped pieces of meat in peppersauce and left them about the yard.

The next day the puppy disappeared. Hari was distressed and felt guilty, but he got some consolation from the film; and when, less than a week later, the puppy returned, dirty, scratched and thinner, Hari embraced him and whispered the words of the film: 'You're my Lassie – my Lassie come home.'

He abandoned all training and was concerned only to see the puppy become healthy again. In the American comic books he read, dogs lived in dog-houses and ate from bowls marked DOG. Hari didn't approve of the dog-houses because they looked small and lonely; but he insisted that his mother should buy a bowl marked DOG.

When he came home for lunch one day she showed him a bowl on which DOG had been painted. Hari's father said he was too hot to eat and went upstairs; his mother followed. Before Hari ate he washed the bowl and filled it with dog-food. He called for the puppy and displayed the bowl. The puppy jumped up, trying to get at the bowl.

Hari put the bowl down and the puppy, instantly ignoring Hari, ran to it. Disappointed, Hari squatted beside the puppy and waited for some sign of recognition. None came. The puppy ate noisily, seeming to catch his food for every chew. Hari passed his hand over the puppy's head.

The puppy, catching a mouthful of food, growled and shook his head.

Hari tried again.

With a sharper growl the puppy dropped the food he had in his mouth and snapped at Hari's hand. Hari felt teeth sinking into his flesh; he could sense the anger driving the teeth, the thought that finally held them back. When he looked at his hand he saw torn skin and swelling blobs of blood. The puppy was bent over the bowl again, catching and chewing, his eyes hard.

Hari seized the bowl marked DOG and threw it with his girl's throw out of the kitchen door. The puppy's growl abruptly ended. When the bowl disappeared he looked up at Hari, puzzled, friendly, his tail swinging slowly. Hari kicked hard at the puppy's muzzle and felt the tip of his shoe striking the bone. The puppy backed away to the door and looked at Hari with bewilderment.

'Come,' Hari said, his voice thick with saliva.

Swinging his tail briskly, the puppy came, passing his neat pink tongue over his black lips, still oily from the food. Hari held out his bitten hand. The puppy licked it clean of blood. Then Hari drove his shoe up against the puppy's belly. He kicked again, but the puppy had run whining out of the kitchen door, and Hari lost his balance and fell. Tears came to his eyes. His hands burned at those points where the puppy's teeth had sunk, and he could still feel the puppy's saliva on his hand, binding the skin.

He got up and went out of the kitchen. The puppy stood by the gate, watching him. Hari bent down, as though to pick up a stone. The puppy made no move. Hari picked up a pebble and flung it at the puppy. It was a clumsy throw and the pebble rose high. The puppy ran to catch it, missed, stopped and stared, his tail swinging, his ears erect, his mouth open. Hari threw another pebble. This one kept low and struck the puppy hard. The puppy whined and ran into the front garden. Hari followed. The puppy ran around the side of the house and hid among the anthurium lilies. Hari aimed one stone after another, and suddenly he had a sense of direction. Again and again he hit the puppy, who whined and ran until he was cornered below the narrow trellis with the Bleeding Heart vine. There he stood still, his eyes restless, his tail between his legs. From time to time he licked his lips. This action infuriated Hari. Blindly he threw stone after stone and the puppy ran from tangle to tangle of Bleeding Heart. Once he tried to rush past Hari, but the way was too narrow and Hari too quick. Hari caught him a drumming kick and he ran back to the corner, watching, faintly whining.

In a choked voice Hari said, 'Come.'

The puppy raised its ears.

Hari smiled and tried to whistle.

Hesitantly, his legs bent, his back curved, the puppy came. Hari stroked his head until the puppy stood erect. Then he held the muzzle with both his hands and squeezed it hard. The puppy yelped and pulled away.

'Hari!' He heard his mother's voice. 'Your father is nearly ready.'

He had had no lunch.

'I have no appetite,' Hari said. They were words his father often used.

She asked about the broken bowl and the food scattered about the yard.

'We were playing,' Hari said.

She saw his hand. 'Those animals don't know their own strength,' she said.

It was his resolve to get the puppy to allow himself to be stroked while eating. Every refusal had to be punished, by beating and stoning, imprisonment in the cupboard below the stairs or imprisonment behind the closed windows of the car, when that was available. Sometimes Hari took the puppy's plate, led the puppy to the lavatory, emptied the plate into the toilet bowl and pulled the flush. Sometimes he threw the food into the yard; then he punished the puppy for eating off the ground. Soon he extended his judgment to all the puppy's actions, punishing those he thought unfriendly, disobedient or ungrateful. If the puppy didn't come to the gate when the car horn sounded, he was to be punished; if he didn't come when called, he was to be punished. Hari kept a careful check of the punishments he had to inflict because he could punish only when his parents were away or occupied, and he was therefore always behindhand. He feared that the puppy might run away again; so he tied him at nights. And when his parents were about, Hari was enraged, as enraged as he had been by that licking of the oily lips, to see the puppy behaving as though unaware of the punishments to come: lying at his father's feet, yawning, curling himself into comfortable positions, or wagging his tail to greet Hari's mother. Sometimes, then, Hari stooped to pick up an imaginary stone, and the puppy ran out of the room. But there were also days when punishments were forgotten, for Hari knew that he controlled the puppy's power and made it an extension of his own, not only by his punishments but also by the complementary hold of affection.

Then came the triumph. The puppy, now almost a dog, attacked Hari one day and had to be pulled back by Hari's parents. 'You can never trust those dogs,' Hari's mother said, and the dog was permanently chained. For days, whenever he could get the chance, Hari beat the dog. One evening, when his parents were out, he beat the dog until it ceased to whine. Then, knowing he was alone, and wishing to test his strength and fear, he unchained the dog. The dog didn't attack, didn't growl. It ran to hide among the anthurium lilies. And after that it allowed itself to be stroked while it ate.

Hari's birthday came again. He was given a Brownie 6-20 camera and wasted film on absurd subjects until his father suggested that a photograph should be taken of Hari and the dog. The dog didn't stand still; eventually they put its collar on and Hari held on to that and smiled for the camera.

Hari's father was busy that Friday and couldn't drive Hari home. Hari stayed at school for the meeting of the Stamp Club and took a taxi home. His father's car was in the drive. He called for the dog. It didn't come. Another punishment. His parents were in the small diningroom next to the kitchen; they sat down to tea. On the dining table Hari saw the yellow folder with the negatives and the prints. They had not come out well. The dog looked strained and awkward, not facing the camera; and Hari thought he himself looked very fat. He felt his parent's eyes on him as he went through the photographs. He turned over one photograph. On the back of it he saw, in his father's handwriting: *In memory of Rex*. Below that was the date.

'It was an accident,' his mother said, putting her arms around him. 'He ran out just as your father was driving in. It was an accident.'

Tears filled Hari's eyes. Sobbing, he stamped up the stairs.

'Mind, son,' his mother called, and Hari heard her say to his father, 'Go after him. His heart. His heart.'

1960

The Baker's Story

Look at me. Black as the Ace of Spades, and ugly to match. Nobody looking at me would believe they looking at one of the richest men in this city of Port-of-Spain. Sometimes I find it hard to believe it myself, you know, especially when I go out on some of the holidays that I start taking the wife and children to these days, and I catch sight of the obzocky black face in one of those fancy mirrors that these expensive hotels have all over the place, as if to spite people like me.

Now everybody – particularly black people – forever asking me how this thing start, and I does always tell them I make my dough from dough. Ha! You like that one? But how it start? Well, you hearing me talk, and I don't have to tell you I didn't have no education. In Grenada, where I come from – and that is one thing these Trinidad black people don't forgive a man for being: a black Grenadian – in Grenada I was one of ten children, I believe – everything kind of mix up out there – and I don't even know who was the feller who hit my mother. I believe he hit a lot of women in all the other parishes of that island, too, because whenever I got back to Grenada for one of those holidays I tell you about, people always telling me that I remind them of this one and that one, and they always mistaking me for a shop assistant whenever I in a shop. (If this thing go on, one day I going to sell somebody something, just for spite.) And even in Trinidad, whenever I run into another Grenadian, the same thing does happen.

Well, I don't know what happen in Grenada, but mammy bring me alone over to Trinidad when she was still young.

I don't know what she do with the others, but perhaps they wasn't even she own. Anyway, she get a work with some white people in St Ann's. They give she a uniform; they give she three meals a day; and they give she a few dollars a month besides. Somehow she get another man, a real Trinidad 'rangoutang, and somehow, I don't know how, she get somebody else to look after me while she was living with this man, for the money and the food she was getting was scarcely enough to support this low-minded Trinidad rango she take up with.

It used to have a Chinee shop not far from this new aunty I was living with, and one day, when the old girl couldn't find the cash no how to buy a bread – is a hell of a thing, come to think of it now, that it have people in this island who can't lay their hands on enough of the ready to buy a bread – well, when she couldn't buy this bread she send me over to this Chinee shop to ask for trust. The Chinee woman – eh, but how these Chinee people does make children! – was big like anything, and I believe I catch she at a good moment, because she say nothing doing, no trust, but if I want a little work that was different, because she want somebody to take some bread she bake for some Indian people. But how she could trust me with the bread? This was a question. And then I pull out my crucifix from under my dirty merino that was more holes than cloth and I tell she to keep it until I come back with the money for the bake bread. I don't know what sort of religion these Chinee people have, but that woman look impressed like anything. But she was smart, though. She keep the crucifix and she send me off with the bread, which was wrap up in a big old *châle-au-pain*, just two or three floursack sew together. I collect the money, bring it back, and she give me back the crucifix with a few cents and a bread.

And that was how this thing really begin. I always tell black people that was God give me my start in life, and don't mind these Trinidadians who does always tell you that Grenadians always praying. Is a true thing, though, because whenever I in any little business difficulty even these days I get down bam! straight on my two knees and I start praying like hell, boy.

Well, so this thing went on, until it was a regular afternoon work for me to deliver people bread. The bakery uses to bake ordinary bread – hops and pan and machine – which they uses to sell to the poorer classes. And how those Chinee people uses to work! This woman, with she big-big belly, clothes all dirty, sweating in front of the oven, making all this bread and making all this money, and I don't know what they doing with it, because all the time they living poor-poor in the back room, with only a bed, some hammocks for the young ones, and a few boxes. I couldn't talk to the husband at all. He didn't know a word of English and all the writing he uses to write uses to be in Chinee. He was a thin nashy feller, with those funny flapping khaki short pants and white merino that Chinee people always wear. He uses to work like a bitch, too. We Grenadians understand hard work, so that is why I suppose I uses to get on so well with these Chinee people, and that is why these lazy black Trinidadians so jealous of we. But was a funny thing. They uses to live so dirty. But the children, man, uses to leave that ramshackle old back room as clean as new bread, and they always had this neatness, always with their little pencil-case and their little rubbers and rulers and blotters, and they never losing anything. They leaving in the morning in one nice little line and in the afternoon they coming back in this same little line, still cool and clean, as though nothing at all touch them all day. Is something they could teach black people children.

But as I was saying this bakery uses to bake ordinary bread for the poorer classes. For the richer classes they uses to bake, too. But what they would do would be to collect the dough from those people house, bake it, and send it back as bread, hot and sweet. I uses to fetch and deliver for this class of customer. They never let me serve in the shop; it was as though they couldn't trust me selling across the counter and collecting money in that rush. Always it had this rush. You know black people: even if it only have one man in the shop he always getting on as if it have one hell of a crowd.

Well, one day when I deliver some bread in this *châle-au-pain* to a family, there was a woman, a neighbour, who start saying how nice it is to get bread which you knead with your own hands and not mix up with all sort of people sweat. And this give me the idea. A oven is a oven. It have to go on, whether it baking one bread or two. So I tell this woman, was a Potogee woman, that I would take she dough and bring it back bake for she, and that it would cost she next to nothing. I say this in a sort of way that she wouldn't know whether I was going to give the money to the Chinee people, or whether it was going to cost she next to nothing because it would be I who was going to take the money. But she give me a look which tell me right away that she wanted me to take the money. So matter fix. So. Back in the *châle-au-pain* the next few days I take some dough, hanging it in the carrier of the bakery bicycle. I take it inside, as though I just didn't bother to wrap up the *châle-au-pain*, and the next thing is that this dough mix up with the other dough, and see me kneading and baking, as though all is one. The thing is, when you go in for a thing like that, to go in brave-brave. It have some people who make so much fuss when they doing one little thing that they bound to get catch. So, and I was surprise like hell, mind you, I get this stuff push in the oven, and is this said Chinee man, always with this sad and sorrowful Chinee face, who pulling it out of the oven with the long-handle shovel, looking at it, and pushing it back in.

And when I take the bread back, with some other bread, I collect the money cool-cool. The thing with a thing like this is that once you start is damn hard to stop. You start calculating this way and that way. And I have a calculating mind. I forever sitting down and working out how much say ·50 a day every day for seven days, and every week for a year, coming to. And so this thing get to be a big thing with me. I wouldn't recommend this to any and everybody who want to go into business. But is what I mean when I tell people that I make my dough by dough.

The Chinee woman wasn't too well now. And the old man was getting on a little funny in a Chinee way. You know how those Chinee fellers does gamble. You drive past Marine Square in the early hours of the Sabbath and is two to one if you don't see some of those Chinee fellers sitting down outside the Treasury, as though they want to be near money, and gambling like hell. Well, the old man was gambling and the old girl was sick, and I was pretty well the only person looking after the bakery. I work damn hard for them, I could tell you. I even pick up two or three words of Chinee, and some of those rude black people start calling me Black Chinee, because at this time I was beginning to dress in short khaki pants and merino like a Chinee and I was drinking that tea Chinee people drinking all day long and I was walking and not saying much like a Chinee. And, now, don't believe what these black people say about Chinee and prejudice, eh. They have nothing at all against black people, provided they is hard-working and grateful.

But life is a funny thing. Now when it look that I all set, that everything going fine and dandy, a whole set of things happen that start me bawling. First, the Chinee lady catch a pleurisy and dead. Was a hell of a thing, but what else you expect when she was always bending down in front of that fire and then getting wet and going out in the dew and everything, and then always making these children too besides. I was sorry like hell, and a little frighten. Because I wasn't too sure how I was going to manage alone with the old man. All the time I work with him he never speak one word straight to me, but he always talking to me through his wife.

And now, look at my crosses. As soon as the woman dead, the Chinee man like he get mad. He didn't cry or anything like that, but he start gambling like a bitch, and the upshot was that one day, perhaps about a month after the old lady dead, the man tell his children to pack up and start leaving, because he gamble and lose the shop to another Chinee feller. I didn't know where I was standing, and nobody telling me nothing. They only packing. I don't know, I suppose they begin to feel that I was just part of the shop, and the old man not even saying that he sorry he lose me. And, you know, as soon as I drop to my knees and start praying, I see it was really God who right from the start put that idea of the dough in my head, because without that I would have been nowhere at all. Because the new feller who take over the shop say he don't want me. He was going to close the bakery and set up a regular grocery, and he didn't want me serving there because the grocery customers wouldn't like black people serving them. So look at me. Twenty-three years old and no work. No nothing. Only I have this Chinee-ness and I know how to bake bread and I have this extra bit of cash I save up over the years.

I slip out of the old khaki short pants and merino and I cruise around the town a little, looking for work. But nobody want bakers. I had about $700.00, and I see that this cruising around would do but it wouldn't pay, because the money was going fast. Now look at this. You know, it never cross my mind in those days that I could open a shop of my own. Is how it is with black people. They get so use to working for other people that they get to believe that because they black they can't do nothing else but work for other people. And I must tell you that when I start praying and God tell me to go out and open a shop for myself I feel that perhaps God did mistake or that I hadn't hear Him good. Because God only saying to me, 'Youngman, take your money and open a bakery. You could bake good bread.' He didn't say to open a parlour, which a few black fellers do, selling rock cakes and mauby and other soft drinks. No, He say open a bakery. Look at my crosses.

I had a lot of trouble borrowing the extra few hundred dollars, but I eventually get a Indian feller to lend me. And this is what I always tell young fellers. That getting credit

ain't no trouble at all if you know exactly what you want to
do. I didn't go round telling people to lend me money because I want to build house or buy lorry. I just did want to
bake bread. Well, to cut a long story short, I buy a break-
down old place near Arouca, and I spend most of what I had
trying to fix the place up. Nothing extravagant, you understand, because Arouca is Arouca and you don't want to
frighten off the country-bookies with anything too sharp.
Too besides, I didn't have the cash. I just put in a few
second-hand glass case and things like that. I write up my
name on a board, and look, I in business.

Now the funny thing happen. In Laventille the people
couldn't have enough of the bread I was baking – and in the
last few months was me was doing the baking. But now
trouble. I baking better bread than the people of Arouca
ever see, and I can't get one single feller to come in like man
through my rickety old front door and buy a penny hops
bread. You hear all this talk about quality being its own
advertisement? Don't believe it, boy. Is quality plus something else. And I didn't have this something else. I begin to
wonder what the hell it could be. I say is because I new in
Arouca that this thing happening. But no. I new, I get stale,
and the people not flocking in their hundreds to the old
shop. Day after day I baking two or three quarts good and all
this just remaining and going dry and stale, and the only
bread I selling is to the man from the government farm, buying
stale cakes and bread for the cows or pigs or whatever they
have up there. And was good bread. So I get down on the
old knees and I pray as though I want to wear them out. And
still I getting the same answer: 'Youngman' – was always
the way I uses to get call in these prayers – 'Youngman, you
just bake bread.'

Pappa! This was a thing. Interest on the loan piling up
every month. Some months I borrow from aunty and anybody else who kind enough to listen just to pay off the
interest. And things get so low that I uses to have to go out
and pretend to people that I was working for another man

bakery and that I was going to bake their dough cheap-cheap. And in Arouca cheap mean cheap. And the little cash I picking up in this disgraceful way was just about enough to keep the wolf from the door, I tell you.

Jeezan. Look at confusion. The old place in Arouca so damn out of the way – was why I did buy it, too, thinking that they didn't have no bakery there and that they would be glad of the good Grenadian-baked – the place so out of the way nobody would want to buy it. It ain't even insure or anything, so it can't get in a little fire accident or anything – not that I went in for that sort of thing. And every time I go down on my knees, the answer coming straight back at me: 'Youngman, you just bake bread.'

Well, for the sake of the Lord I baking one or two quarts regular every day, though I begin to feel that the Lord want to break me, and I begin to feel too that this was His punishment for what I uses to do to the Chinee people in their bakery. I was beginning to feel bad and real ignorant. I uses to stay away from the bakery after baking those quarts for the Lord – nothing to lock up, nothing to thief – and, when any of the Laventille boys drop in on the way to Manzanilla and Balandra and those other beaches on the Sabbath, I uses to tell them, making a joke out of it, that I was 'loafing'. They uses to laugh like hell, too. It have nothing in the whole world so funny as to see a man you know flat out on his arse and catching good hell.

The Indian feller was getting anxious about his cash, and you couldn't blame him, either, because some months now he not even seeing his interest. And this begin to get me down, too. I remember how all the man did ask me when I went to him for money was: 'You sure you want to bake bread? You feel you have a hand for baking bread?' And yes-yes, I tell him, and just like that he shell out the cash. And now he was getting anxious. So one day, after baking those loaves for the Lord, I take a Arima Bus Service bus to Port-of-Spain to see this feller. I was feeling brave enough on the way. But as soon as I see the old sea and get a whiff of South

Quay and the bus touch the Railway Station terminus my belly start going pweh-pweh. I decide to roam about the city for a little.

Was a hot morning, *petit-carême* weather, and in those days a coconut uses still to cost ·04. Well, it had this coconut cart in the old square and I stop by it. It was a damn funny thing to see. The seller was a black feller. And you wouldn't know how funny this was, unless you know that every coconut seller in the island is Indian. They have this way of handling a cutlass that black people don't have. Coconut in left hand; with right hand bam, bam, bam with cutlass, and coconut cut open, ready to drink. I ain't never see a coconut seller chop his hand. And here was this black feller doing this bam-bam business on a coconut with a cutlass. It was as funny as seeing a black man wearing dhoti and turban. The sweetest part of the whole business was that this black feller was, forgetting looks, just like a Indian. He was talking Hindustani to a lot of Indian fellers, who was giving him jokes like hell, but he wasn't minding. It does happen like that sometimes with black fellers who live a lot with Indians in the country. They putting away curry, talking Indian, and behaving just like Indians. Well, I take a coconut from this black man and then went on to see the feller about the money.

He was more sad than vex when I tell him, and if I was in his shoes I woulda be sad, too. Is a hell of a thing when you see your money gone and you ain't getting the sweet little kisses from the interest every month. Anyway, he say he would give me three more months' grace, but that if I didn't start shelling out at the agreed rate he would have to foreclose. 'You put me in a hell of a position,' he say. 'Look at me. You think I want a shop in Arouca?'

I was feeling a little better when I leave the feller, and who I should see when I leave but Percy. Percy was a old rango who uses to go to the Laventille elementary school with me. I never know a boy get so much cut-arse as Percy. But he grow up real hard and ignorant with it, and now he wearing fancy clothes like a saga boy, and talking about

various business offers. I believe he was selling insurance –
is a thing that nearly every idler doing in Trinidad, and,
mark my words, the day coming when you going to see those
fellers trying to sell insurance to one another. Anyway,
Percy getting on real flash, and he say he want to stand me
a lunch for old times' sake. He make a few of the usual ignorant Trinidadian jokes about Grenadians, and we went up
to the Angostura Bar. I did never go there before, and
wasn't the sort of place you would expect a rango like Percy
to be welcome. But we went up there and Percy start throwing his weight around with the waiters, and, mind you, they
wasn't even a quarter as black as Percy. Is a wonder they
didn't abuse him, especially with all those fair people
around. After the drinks Percy say, 'Where you want to have
this lunch?'

Me, I don't know a thing about the city restaurants, and
when Percy talk about food all I was expecting was rice and
peas or a roti off a Indian stall or a mauby and rock cake in
some parlour. And is a damn hard thing to have people, even
people as ignorant as Percy, showing off on you, especially
when you carrying two nails in your pocket to make the
jingling noise. So I tell Percy we could go to a parlour or a
bar. But he say, 'No, no. When I treat my friends, I don't
like black people meddling with my food.'

And was only then that the thing hit me. I suppose that
what Trinidadians say about the stupidness of Grenadians
have a little truth, though you have to live in a place for a
long time before you get to know it really well. Then the
thing hit me, man.

When black people in Trinidad go to a restaurant they
don't like to see black people meddling with their food. And
then I see that though Trinidad have every race and every
colour, every race have to do special things. But look, man.
If you want to buy a snowball, who you buying it from?
You wouldn't buy it from a Indian or a Chinee or a Potogee.
You would buy it from a black man. And I myself, when I
was getting my place in Arouca fix up, I didn't employ

Indian carpenters or masons. If a Indian in Trinidad decide to go into the carpentering business the man would starve. Who ever see a Indian carpenter? I suppose the only place in the world where they have Indian carpenters and Indian masons is India. Is a damn funny thing. One of these days I must make a trip to that country, to just see this thing. And as we walking I see the names of bakers: Coelho, Pantin, Stauble. Potogee or Swiss, or something, and then all those other Chinee places. And, look at the laundries. If a black man open a laundry, you would take your clothes to it? *I* wouldn't take my clothes there. Well, I walking to this restaurant, but I jumping for joy. And then all sorts of things fit into place. You remember that the Chinee people didn't let me serve bread across the counter? I uses to think it was because they didn't trust me with the rush. But it wasn't that. It was that, if they did let me serve, they would have had no rush at all. You ever see anybody buying their bread off a black man?

I ask Percy why he didn't like black people meddling with his food in public places. The question throw him a little. He stop and think and say, 'It don't *look* nice.'

Well, you could guess the rest of the story. Before I went back to Arouca that day I make contact with a yellow boy call Macnab. This boy was half black and half Chinee, and, though he had a little brown colour and the hair a little curly, he could pass for one of those Cantonese. They a little darker than the other Chinee people, I believe. Macnab I find beating a steel pan in somebody yard – they was practising for Carnival – and I suppose the only reason that Macnab was willing to come all the way to Arouca was because he was short of the cash to buy his costume for the Carnival band.

But he went up with me. I put him in front of the shop, give him a merino and a pair of khaki short pants, and tell him to talk as Chinee as he could, if he wanted to get that Carnival bonus. I stay in the back room, and I start baking bread. I even give Macnab a old Chinee paper, not to read, because Macnab could scarcely read English, but just to leave lying around, to make it look good. And I get hold of one of those big Chinee calendars with Chinee women and flowers and waterfalls and hang it up on the wall. And when this was all ready, I went down on my knees and thank God. And still the old message coming, but friendly and happy now: 'Youngman, you just bake bread.'

And, you know, that solve another problem. I was worrying to hell about the name I should give the place. New Shanghai, Canton, Hongkong, Nanking, Yang-tse-Kiang. But when the old message come over I know right away what the name should be. I scrub off the old name – no need to tell you what that was – and I get a proper sign painter to copy a few letters from the Chinee newspaper. Below that, in big letters, I make him write:

YUNG MAN
BAKER

I never show my face in the front of the shop again. And I tell you, without boasting, that I bake damn good bread. And the people of Arouca ain't that foolish. They know a good thing. And soon I was making so much money that I was able to open a branch in Arima and then another in Port-of-Spain self. Was hard in the beginning to get real Chinee people to work for a black man. But money have it own way of talking, and when today you pass any of the Yung Man establishments all you seeing behind the counter is Chinee. Some of them ain't even know they working for a black man. My wife handling that side of the business, and the wife is Chinee. She come from down Cedros way. So look at me now, in Port-of-Spain, giving Stauble and Pantin and Coelho a run for their money. As I say, I only going in the shops from the back. But every Monday morning I walking brave brave to Marine Square and going in the bank, from the front.

1962

A Flag on the Island

A Fantasy for a Small Screen

I

It was an island around which I had been circling for some years. My duties often took me that way and I could have called there any time. But in my imagination the island had ceased to be accessible; and I wanted it to remain so. A lassitude always fell upon me whenever – working from the name made concrete and ordinary on say an airport board – I sought to recreate a visit. So easy then to get into a car, to qualify a name with trees, houses, people, their quaint advertisements and puzzling journeys. So easy to destroy more than a name. All landscapes are in the end only in the imagination; to be faced with the reality is to start again.

And now the island was upon me. It was not on our itinerary. But out there, among the tourist isles to the north, there was the big annual event of the hurricanes; and it was news of one of these hurricanes, called Irene, that was making us put in. The island, we were told in the ship's bulletin, was reasonably safe. There had been a hurricane here, and a mild one, only once, in the 1920s; and scientists at that time had said, in the way scientists have, that the island was safe for another hundred years. You wouldn't have thought so, though, from the excitement in the announcements from the local radio station, which our transistors had begun to pick up as we came slowly into the harbour through the narrow channel, still and clear and dangerous, between tall green-thatched rocky islets.

Channel and islets which I had never hoped or wished to see again. Still there. And I had been so calm throughout the journey northwards. Abstemiousness, even self-mortification, had settled on me almost as soon as I had gone aboard; and had given me a deep content. I had been eating little and drinking not at all. I fancied that I was shrinking from day to day, and this daily assessment had been pleasing. When I sat I tried to make myself as small as possible; and it had been a pleasure to me then to put on my spectacles and to attempt to read, to be the ascetic who yet knew the greater pleasure of his own shrinking flesh. To be the ascetic, to be mild and gentle and soft-spoken, withdrawn and ineffectual; to have created for oneself that little clearing in the jungle of the mind; and constantly to reassure oneself that the clearing still existed.

Now as we moved into the harbour I could feel the jungle press in again. I was jumpy, irritated, unsatisfied, suddenly incomplete. Still, I made an effort. I decided not to go ashore with the others. We were to stay on the island until the hurricane had blown itself out. The shipping company had arranged trips and excursions.

'What's the name of this place? They always give you the name of the place in airports. Harbours try to keep you guessing. I wonder why?'

'Philosopher!'

Husband and wife, playing as a team.

Already we were news. On the transistors there came a new announcement, breathless like the others: 'Here is an appeal from the Ministry of Public Order and Education. Five hundred tourists will be on our island for the next few days. The Ministry urges that these tourists be treated with our customary courtesy and kindness.'

'The natives are excited,' a tourist said to me.

'Yes,' I said, 'I think there is a good chance they will eat us. We look pretty appetizing.'

Red dust hung in a cloud above the bauxite loading station, disfiguring the city and the hills. The tourists gazed, lining the rails in bermuda shorts, bright cotton shirts and straw hats. They looked vulnerable.

'Here is an appeal from the Ministry of Public Order and Education. . . .'

I imagined the appeal going to the barbershops, rumshops, cafés and back-yards of the ramshackle town I had known.

The radio played a commercial for a type of shirt; an organ moaned and some deaths were announced; there was a commercial for a washing powder; then the time was tremendously announced and there were details of weather and temperature.

A woman said, 'They get worked up about the time and the weather here too.'

Her husband, his bitterness scarcely disguised by the gaiety of his tourist costume, said, 'Why the hell shouldn't they?'

They were not playing as a team.

I went down to my cabin. On the way I ran into the happier team, already dressed as for a carnival.

'You're not going ashore?' asked the male.

'No. I think I will just stay here and read.'

And in my self-imposed isolation, I did try to read. I put on my spectacles and tried to savour my shrinking, mortified flesh. But it was no use; the jungle pressed; confusion and threat were already being converted into that internal excitement which is in itself fulfilment, and exhaustion.

Here on this Moore-McCormack liner everything was Moore-McCormack. In my white cabin the name called to me from every corner, from every article, from towels, from toilet paper, from writing paper, from table cloth, from pillow-cases, from bed sheets, from blankets, from cups and menus. So that the name appeared to have gone deep, to have penetrated, like the radiation we have been told to fear, the skin of all those exposed to it, to have shaped itself in living red corpuscles within bodies.

Moore-McCormack, Moore-McCormack. Man had become God. Impossible in this cabin to escape; yet I knew that once we were out of the ship the name would lose its power. So that my decision was almost made for me. I would go ashore; I would spend the night ashore. My mood was on me; I let it settle; I let it take possession of me. Then I saw that I too, putting away briefcase, papers, letters, passport, was capable of my own feeble assertions. I too had tried to give myself labels, and none of my labels could convince me that I belonged to myself.

This is part of my mood; it heightens my anxiety; I feel the whole world is being washed away and that I am being washed away with it. I feel my time is short. The child, testing his courage, steps into the swiftly moving stream, and though the water does not go above his ankles, in an instant the safe solid earth vanishes, and he is aware only of the terror of sky and trees and the force at his feet. Split seconds of lucidity add to his terror. So, we can use the same toothpaste for years and end by not seeing the colour of the tube; but set us among strange labels, set us in disturbance, in an unfamiliar landscape; and every unregarded article we possess becomes isolated and speaks of our peculiar dependence.

'You are going to spend the night ashore?'

The question came from a small intelligent-looking man with a round, kind face. He had been as withdrawn from the life of the ship as myself, and I had always seen him in the company of a big grey-suited man whose face I had never been able to commit to memory. I had heard rumours that he was very rich, but I had paid no attention; as I had paid no attention to the other rumour that we had a Russian spy on board as a prisoner.

'Yes, I am going to be brave.'

'Oh, I am glad,' he said, 'we are going to have lots of fun together.'

'Thanks for asking me.'

'When I say fun, I don't mean what you mean.'

'I don't know what you mean either.'

He did not stop smiling. 'I imagine that you are going ashore for pleasure.'

'Well, I suppose that you could call it that.'

'I am glad we put in here.' His expression became that of
a man burdened by duty. 'You see I have a little business to
do here.' He spoke gravely, but his excitement was clear.
'Do you know the island?'

'I used to know it very well.'

'Well, I am so glad we have met. You are just the sort of
person I want to meet. You could be of great help to me.'

'I can simplify matters for you by giving you a list of
places you must on no account go to.'

He looked pained. 'I am really here on business.'

'You can do good business here. I used to.'

Pleasure? I was already exhausted. My stomach felt tight;
and all the unexpended energy of days, of weeks, seemed to
have turned sour. Already the craving for shellfish and seafood was on me. I could almost feel its sick stale taste in my
mouth, and I knew that for all that had happened in the past,
I would eat no complete meal for some time ahead, and that
while my mood lasted the pleasures I looked for would
quickly turn to a distressing-satisfying endurance test,
would end by being pain.

I had been the coldest of tourists, unexcited by the unexpected holiday. Now, as we landed, I was among the most
eager.

'Hey, that was a pretty quick read.'

'I read the last page – the butler did it.'

In the smart reception building, well-groomed girls, full of
selfconscious charm, chosen for race and colour, with one or
two totally, diplomatically black, pressed island souvenirs on
us: toy steel-drums, market-woman dolls in cotton, musicians
in wire, totem-like faces carved from coconuts. Beyond the
wire-netting fence, the taxi drivers of the city seethed. It
seemed a frail barrier.

'It's like the zoo,' the woman said.

'Yes,' said her embittered husband. 'They might even
throw you some nuts.'

I looked for a telephone. I asked for a directory. It was a
small directory.

'A toy directory,' the happy tourist said.

'It's full of the numbers of dolls,' I said.

I dialled, I waited. A voice I knew said, 'Hullo.' I closed my eyes to listen. The voice said, 'Hullo, hullo.' I put the receiver down.

'Naughty.'

It was my friend from the ship. His companion stood at the other end of the room, his back to us; he was looking at books on a revolving bookstand.

'What do you think Sinclair is interested in? Shall we go and see?'

We moved over. Sinclair shuffled off.

Most of the books displayed were by a man called H. J. B. White. The back of each book had a picture of the author. A tormented writer's-photograph face. But I imagined it winking at me. I winked back.

'Do you know him?' my friend asked.

'I don't know whether any of us really knew Mr Black-white,' I said. 'He was a man who moved with the times.'

'Local writer?'

'Very local.'

He counted the titles with an awed finger. 'He looks tremendous. Oh, I hope I can see him. Oh, this looks very good.'

The book he picked up was called *I Hate You*, with the sub-title *One Man's Search for Identity*. He opened the book greedily and began moving his lips, ' "I am a man without identity. Hate has consumed my identity. My personality has been distorted by hate. My hymns have not been hymns of praise, but of hate. How terrible to be Caliban, you say. But I say, how tremendous. Tremendousness is therefore my unlikely subject." '

He stopped reading, held the book out to the assistant and said, 'Miss, Miss, I would like to buy this.' Then, indicating one title after the other: 'And this, and this, and this, and this.'

He was not the only one. Many of the tourists had been deftly guided to the bookstall.

'Native author.'

'Don't use that word.'

'Lots of local colour, you think?'

'Mind your language.'

'But look, he's attacking us.'

'No, he's only attacking tourists.'

The group moved on, leaving a depleted shelf.

I bought all H. J. B. White's books.

The girl who sold them to me said, 'Tourists usually go for *I Hate You*, but I prefer the novels myself. They're heartwarming stories.'

'Good clean sex?'

'Oh no, inter-racial.'

'Sorry, I need another language.'

I put on my spectacles and read on the dedication page of one book: 'Thanks are due to the Haaker Foundation whose generous support facilitated the composition of this work.' Another book offered thanks to the Stockwell Foundation. My companion – he was becoming my companion – held all his own books under his arm and read with me from mine.

'You see,' he said, 'they're all after him. I don't imagine he'll want to look at me.'

We were given miniature rum bottles with the compliments of various firms. Little leaflets and folders full of photographs and maps with arrows and X's told us of the beauties of the island, now fully charted. The girl was especially friendly when she explained about the sights.

'You have mud volcanoes here,' I said, 'and that's pretty good. But the leaflet doesn't say. Which is the best whorehouse in town nowadays?'

Tourists stared. The girl called: 'Mr Phillips.' And my companion held my arm, smiled as to a child and said soothingly: 'Hey, I believe I am going to have to look after you. I know how it is when things get on top of you.'

'You know, I believe you do.'

'My name's Leonard.'

'I am Frank,' I said.

'Short for Frankenstein. Forget it, that's my little joke. And you see my friend over there, but you can't see his face? His name's Sinclair.'

Sinclair stood, with his back to us, studying some tormented paintings of black beaches below stormy skies.

'But Sinclair won't talk to you, especially now that he's seen me talking to you.'

In the turmoil of the reception building we were three fixed points.

'Why won't Sinclair talk to me?'

'He's jealous.'

'Hooray for you.'

I broke away to get a taxi.

'Hey, you can't leave me. I'm worried about you, remember?'

Below a wooden arch that said WELCOME TO THE COLOURFUL ISLAND the taxi drivers, sober in charcoal-grey trousers, white shirts, some even with ties, behaved like people maddened by the broadcast pleas for courtesy. They rushed the tourists, easy targets in their extravagantly Caribbean cottons stamped with palm-fringed beaches, thatched huts and grass skirts. The tropics appeared to be on their backs alone; when they got into their taxis the tropics went with them.

We came out into an avenue of glass buildings, airconditioned bars, filling stations and snappily worded advertisements. The slogan PRIDE, TOIL, CULTURE, was everywhere. There was a flag over the customs building. It was new to me: rays from a yellow sun lighting up a wavy blue sea.

'What did you do with the Union Jack?'

The taxi driver said, 'They take it away, and they send this. To tell the truth I prefer the old Union Jack. Now don't misunderstand me, I talking about the flag as a flag. They send us this thing and they try to sweeten us up with some old talk about *or, a pile gules, argenta bordure, barry-wavy*. They try to sweeten us up with that, but I prefer the old Union Jack. It look like a real flag. This look like something they make up. You know, like foreign money?'

Once the island had seemed to me flagless. There was the Union Jack of course, but it was a remote affirmation. The island was a floating suspended place to which you brought your own flag if you wanted to. Every evening on the base we used to pull down the Stars and Stripes at sunset; the bugle would sound and through the city of narrow streets, big trees and old wooden houses, every American serviceman would stand to attention. It was a ridiculous affirmation – the local children mocked us – but only one in a city of ridiculous affirmations. For a long time Mr Blackwhite had a coloured portrait of Haile Selassie in his front room; and in his corner grocery Ma-Ho had a photograph of Chiang Kai-shek between his Chinese calendars. On the flagless island we, saluting the flag, were going back to America; Ma-Ho was going back to Canton as soon as the war was over; and the picture of Haile Selassie was there to remind Mr Black-white, and to remind us, that he too had a place to go back to. 'This place doesn't exist,' he used to say, and he was wiser than any of us.

Now, driving through the city whose features had been so altered, so that alteration seemed to have spread to the land itself, the nature of the soil, I felt again that the reality of landscape and perhaps of all relationships lay only in the imagination. The place existed now: that was the message of the flag.

The road began to climb. On a culvert two calypsonians, dressed for the part, sat disconsolately waiting for custom. A little later we saw two who had been successful. They were serenading the happy wife. The taxi driver, hands in pockets, toothpick in mouth, stood idle. The embittered husband stood equally idle, but he was like a man fighting an inward rage.

The hotel was new. There were murals in the lobby which sought to exalt the landscape and the people which the hotel's very existence seemed to deny. The noticeboard in the lobby gave the name of our ship and added: 'Sailing

Indefinite'. A poster advertised The Coconut Grove. Another announced a Barbecue Night at the Hilton, Gary Priestland, popular TV personality, Master of Ceremonies. A photograph showed him with his models. But I saw only Priest, white-robed Priest, handler of the language, handler of his six little hymn-singing girls. He didn't wink at me. He scowled; he threatened. I covered his face with my hand.

In my moods I tell myself that the world is not being washed away; that there is time; that the blurring of fantasy with reality which gives me the feeling of helplessness exists only in my mind. But then I know that the mind is alien and unfriendly, and I am never able to regulate things. Hilton, Hilton. Even here, even in the book on the bedside table. And The Coconut Grove again in a leaflet on the table, next to the bowl of fruit in green cellophane tied with a red ribbon.

I telephoned for a drink; then I telephoned again to hear the voice and to say nothing. Even before lunch I had drunk too much.

'Frank, your eye is still longer than your tongue.'

It was an island saying; I thought I could hear the words on the telephone.

Lunch, lunch. Let it be ordered in every sense. Melon or avocado to start, something else to follow – but what? But what? And as soon as I entered the diningroom the craving for oysters and shellfish became overpowering. The liveried page strolled through the diningroom beating a toy steel pan and calling out a name. I fancied it was mine: 'Frankie, Frankie.' But of course I knew better.

I saw Sinclair's back as he walked to a table. He sat at the far end like a man controlling the panorama.

'Are you feeling better?'

'Leonard?'

'Frank.'

'Do you like seafood, Leonard?'

'In moderation.'

'I am going to have some oysters.'

'A good starter. Let's have some, I'll have half a dozen.'

The waiter carried the emblem of yellow sun and wavy sea on his lapel; my eyes travelled down those waves.

'Half a dozen oysters for him. Fifty for me.'

'Fifty,' Leonard said.

'Well, let's make it a hundred.'

Leonard smiled. 'Boy, I'm glad I met you. You believe me, don't you, Frank?'

'I believe you.'

'You know, people don't believe I have come here to work. They think I am making it up.'

The waiter brought Leonard his six oysters and brought me my hundred. The oysters were of the tiny island variety; six scarcely filled one indentation of Leonard's oyster plate.

'Are these six oysters?' Leonard asked the waiter.

'They are six oysters.'

'Okay, okay,' Leonard said soothingly, 'I just wanted to find out. Of course,' he said to me, 'it doesn't sound like work. You see – '

And here the liveried page walked back through the dining-room beating a bright tune on his toy pan and calling out a name.

' – you see, I have got to give away a million dollars.'

My oysters had come in a tumbler. I scooped up about a dozen and swallowed them.

'Exactly,' Leonard said. 'It doesn't sound like work. But it is. One wants to be sure that one is using the money sensibly. It's easy enough to make a million dollars, I always say. Much harder to spend it.'

'That's what I have always felt. Excuse me.'

I went up to my room. The oysters had been too many for me. The sick tightness was in my stomach. Even at this early stage it was necessary for me to drive myself on.

I was careful, as I always am on these occasions, to prepare sensibly. I lined the waist-band of my trousers with the new funny island money; I distributed notes all over my pockets; I even lay some flat in my shoes.

A letter from home among my papers. Nothing important;

no news; just a little bit about the drains, the wonderful workmen who had helped. Brave girl. Brave.

I remembered again. I lifted the telephone, asked for a line, dialled. The same voice answered and again my courage left me and I listened to the squawks until the phone went dead.

I had stripped myself of all my labels, of all my assertions. Soon I would be free. Hilton, Hilton: man as God. Goodbye to that now. My excitement was high.

I went to the desk, transferred a fixed sum to the hotel vault. The final fraudulence that we cannot avoid: we might look for escape, but we are always careful to provide for escape from that escape.

While the clerk was busy I took the pen from the desk, blacked out the whites of Gary Priestland's eyes and sent an arrow through his neck. The clerk was well trained. It was only after I had turned that he removed the disfigured poster and replaced it by a new one.

The liveried doorman whistled up a taxi. I gave him a local dollar; too much, but I enjoyed his attempt to look unsurprised. He opened the taxi door, closed it, saluted. It was the final moment of responsibility. I did not give the taxi driver the name of any bar; I gave him the name of a department store in the centre of the city. And when I got off I actually went into the store, as though the taxi driver was watching me and it was important that I should not step out of the character which he must have built up for me.

The store was airconditioned. The world was cool and muffled. My irritation was sharpened.

'Can I help you, sir?'

'No thank you, I am just passing through.'

I spoke with unnecessary aggressiveness; one or two customers stared and I instinctively waited for Leonard's interjection.

'Leonard,' I whispered, turning.

But he wasn't there.

The shop girl took a step backwards and I hurried out through the other door into the shock of damp heat, white light, and gutter smells. Hooray for airconditioning. My mood had taken possession of me. I was drunk on more, and on less, than alcohol.

The money began to leak out of my fingers. This is part of the excitement; money became paper over which other people fought. Two dollars entrance here; one dollar for a beer there; cigarettes at twice the price: I paid in paper. Bright rooms, killing bright, and noisy as the sea. The colours yellow, green, red, on drinks, labels, calendars on the walls. On the television, intermittently through a series of such bars, Gary Priestland, chairing a discussion on love and marriage. And from a totally black face, a woman's, black enough to be featureless, issued: 'Well, I married for love.' 'No, she married for hate.' Laughter was like the sea. Someone played with the knob on the set; and the thought, perhaps expressed, came to me: 'It is an unkind medium.'

In bright rooms, bright seas, I floated. And I explored dark caves, so dark you groped and sat still and in the end you found that you were alone.

'Where is everybody?'

'They are coming just now.'

In an almost empty room – dim lights, dark walls, dark chairs – the man sitting at the edge of the table invited us to come close up to him. We all six in the room moved up to him, as to a floor show. He crossed his legs and swung them. 'Is he going to strip?'

Confusion again. The door; the tiled entrance; the discreet board:

BRITISH COUNCIL
The Elizabethan Lyric
A Course of Six Lectures

I always feel it would be so much better if I could wait to pick and choose. Time after time I promise myself to do so. But when the girl came and said – so sad it seemed to me – 'I am going to screw you,' I knew that this was how it would begin; that I wouldn't have the will to resist.

PRIDE, flashed the neon light across the square.

She ordered a stout.

'You are an honest girl.'

'Stout does build me up.'

TOIL

The stout came.

'Ah,' she said, 'my old bulldog.'

And from the neck label the bulldog growled at me. With the stout there also came two men dressed like calypsonians in the travel brochures, dressed like those calypsonians on the climbing road to the hotel.

'Allow me to welcome the gentleman to our colourful island.'

CULTURE

'Get away,' I shouted.

She looked a little nervous; she nodded uncertainly to someone behind me and said, 'Is all right, Percy.' Then to me: 'Why you driving them away?'

'They embarrass me.'

'How you mean, they embarrass you?'

'They're not real. Look, I could put my hand through them.'

The man with the guitar lifted his arm; my hand went through.

The song went on: 'In two-twos, this gentleman got the alcoholic blues.'

'God!'

When I uncovered my face I saw a ringed hand before it. It was an expectant hand. I paid; I drank.

A fat white woman began to do a simple little dance on the raised floor. I couldn't look.

'What wrong with you?'

And when the woman made as if to discard the final garment, I stood up and shouted. 'No!'

'But how a big man like you could shame me so?'

The man who had been sitting with a stick at the top of the steps came to our table. He waved around the room, past paintings of steel-bands and women dancing on golden sand, and pointed to a sign:

Patrons are requested to abstain from
lewd and offensive gestures
By order, Ministry of Order and Public Education

'Is all right, Percy,' the girl said.

Percy could only point. Speech was out of the question because of the steel orchestra. I sat down.

Percy went away and the girl said gently: 'Sit down and tell me why you finding everything embarrassing. What else you tourists come here for?' She beckoned to the waitress. 'I want a fry chicken.'

'No,' I said. 'No damn fry chicken for you.'

At that moment the band stopped, and my words filled the room. The Japanese sailors – we had seen their trawlers in the harbour – looked up. The American airmen looked up. Percy looked up.

And in the silence the girl shouted to the room, 'He finding everything embarrassing, and he damn mean with it.' She stood up and pointed at me. 'He travelling all over the world. And all I want is a fry chicken.'

'Frank,' I heard a voice whisper.

'Leonard,' I whispered back.

'O boy, I am glad I've found you. I've had such a time looking for you. I have been in so many different bars, so many. I've got all these nice names, all these interesting people I've got to assist and give money to. Sometimes I had trouble getting the names. You know how people misunderstand. I was worried about you. Sinclair was worried about you too.'

Sinclair was sitting at a table in the distance with his back to us, drinking.

Caught between Leonard and a demand for fried chicken, I bought the fried chicken.

'You know,' Leonard said confidentially, 'it seems that the place to go to is The Coconut Grove. It sounds terrific, just what I am looking for. You know it?'

'I know it.'

'Well look, why don't we all three of us just go there now.'

'Not me at The Coconut Grove,' the girl said.

Leonard said to me, 'I meant you and me and Sinclair.'

'What the hell you mean?' She stood up and held the bottle of stout at an angle over Leonard's head, as though ready to pour. She called, 'Percy!'

Leonard closed his eyes, passive and expectant.

'I'll be with you in a minute, Leonard,' I said, and I ran down the steps with the girl who was still holding the bottle of stout.

'How you get so impatient so sudden?'

'I don't know, but this is your big chance.'

The open car door at the foot of the steps was like an invitation. We got in, the door slammed behind us.

'I've got to get away from those people upstairs. They're mad, they're quite mad. You don't know what I rescued you from.'

She looked at me.

So it began: the walking out past tables; the casual stares; the refusal to walk the hundred yards to the hotel; the two-dollar taxi; the unswept concrete steps; the dimly lit rooms; the cheap wooden furniture; the gaudy calendars on the wall, mocking desire, mocking flesh; the blue shimmer of television screens; Gary Priestland, now with the news of the hurricane; the startling gentility of glass cabinets; the much-used bed.

And in lucid intermissions, the telephone: the squawks, the slams.

So it began. The bars, the hotels, pointless conversations with girls. 'What's your name? Where do you come from? What do you want?' The drinks; the bloated feeling in the stomach; the sick taste of island oysters and red pepper sauce; the airless rooms; the wastepaper baskets, wetly and whitely littered; and white wash-basins which, supine on stale beds, one associated with hospitals, medicines, operations, feverishness, delirium.

'No!'

'But I ain't even touch you yet.'

Above me a foolish face, the poor body offering its charms that were no charms. Poor body; poor flesh; poor man.

And again confusion. I must have spoken the words. A woman wailed, claiming insult and calling for brave men, and the bare wooden staircase resounded. Then among trellis and roses, dozens of luminous white roses, a dog barked, and growled. The offended black body turned white with insult. The same screams, the same call for vengeance. Down an aisle, between hundreds and hundreds of fully clothed men with spectacles and pads and pencils, the body chased me. To another entrance; another tiled floor; another discreet board:

ALLIANCE FRANÇAISE
Art Course
Paris Model
(Admission free)

And the glimpses of Leonard: like scenes imagined, the man with the million dollars to give away, the Pied Piper whom as in a dream I saw walking down the street followed by processions of steel-bandsmen, singers, and women calling for his money. At the head he walked, benign, stunned, smiling.

The day had faded, the night moved in jerks, in great swallows of hours. Lighted clocks had wise and patient faces.

The bar smelled of rum and latrines. The beer and some notes and some silver were pushed at me through the gap in the wire-netting. My right hand was gripped and the black face, smiling, menacing, humorous, frightening, which I seemed to study pore by pore, hair by hair, was saying, 'Leave the change for me, nuh.'

Confusion. Glimpses of faces expressing interest rather than hostility. A tumbling and a rumbling; a wet floor; my own shouts of 'No', and the repeated answering sentence: 'Next time you walk with money.'

And in the silent street off the deserted square, midnight

approaching, the Cinderella hour, I was sitting on the pavement, totally lucid, with my feet in the gutter, sucking an orange. Sitting below the old straw-hatted lady, lit by the yellow smoking flame of a bottle flambeau. On the television in the shop window, Gary Priestland and the Ma-Ho Four, frantic and mute behind plate-glass.

'Better?' she said.

'Better.'

'These people nowadays, they never have, they only want.'

'What do they want?'

'What you have. Look.'

The voice was mock American: 'Man, I can get anything for you?'

'What do you have?'

'I have white,' the taxi driver said. 'I have Chinese, I have Portuguese, I have Indian, I have Spanish. Don't ask me for black. I don't do black.'

'That's right, boy,' the old lady said. 'Keep them out of mischief.'

'I couldn't do black or white now.'

'Was what I was thinking,' the orange lady said.

'Then you want The Coconut Grove,' the taxi driver said. 'Very cultural. All the older shots go there.'

'You make it sound very gay.'

'I know what you mean. This culture would do, but it wouldn't pay. Is just a lot of provocation if you ask me. A lot of wicked scanty clothing and all you doing with your two hands at the end is clapping. The spirit of the older shots being willing, but the flesh being weak.'

'That sounds like me. After mature consideration I think we will go to The Coconut Grove.'

'And too besides, I was going to say, they wouldn't take you in like this, old man. Look at you.'

'I don't know, I believe I have lost you somewhere. Do you want me to go to this place?'

'I don't want nothing. I was just remarking that they wouldn't take you in.'

'Let's try.'

'In these cultural joints they have big bouncers, you know.'

We drove through silent streets in which occasionally neon lights flashed PRIDE, TOIL, CULTURE. On the car radio came the news of midnight. Terrific news, from the way it was presented. Then came news of wind velocity and temperature, and of the hurricane, still out there.

'You see what I mean,' the taxi driver said when we stopped.

'It has changed,' I said. 'It used to be an ordinary house, you know. You know those wooden houses with gables and fretwork along the eaves?'

'Oh, the old-fashioned ones. We are pulling them down all the time now. You mustn't think a lot of them still remain.'

Henry's was new and square, with much glass. Behind the glass, potted greenery; and behind that, blinds. Rough stone walls, recessed mortar, a heavy glass door, heavy, too, with recommendations from clubs and travel associations, like the suitcase of an old-fashioned traveller. And behind the door, the bouncer.

'Big, eh?' the taxi driver said.

'He's a big man.'

'You want to try your luck?'

'Perhaps a little later. Just now I just want you to drive slowly down the street.'

The bouncer watched us move off. I looked back at him; he continued to look at me. And how could I have forgotten? Opposite The Coconut Grove, what? I looked. I saw.

Ministry of Order and Public Education
University College
Creative Writing Department
Principal: H. J. B. White
Grams: Olympus

'You don't mind going so slowly?' I asked the driver.

'No, I do a lot of funeral work when I'm not hustling.'

No overturned dustbins on the street now; no pariah dogs timidly pillaging. The street we moved down was like a street in an architect's drawing. Above the neat new buildings trees tossed. The wind was high; the racing clouds were black and silver. We came to an intersection.

'Supermarket,' the driver said, pointing.

'Supermarket.'

A little further on my anxiety dissolved. Where I had expected and feared to find a house, there was an empty lot. I got out of the car and went to look.

'What are you looking for?' the taxi driver asked.

'My house.'

'You sure you left it here? That was a damn careless thing to do.'

'They've pulled down my house.' I walked among the weeds, looking.

'The house not here,' the taxi-driver said. 'What you looking for?'

'An explanation. Here, go, leave me alone.' I paid him off.

He didn't go. He remained where he was and watched me. I began to walk briskly back towards The Coconut Grove, the wind blowing my hair, making my shirt flap, and it seemed that it was just in this way, though not at night and under a wild sky, but in broad daylight, below a high light sky, that I had first come to this street. The terror of sky and trees, the force at my feet.

II

I used to feel in those days that it was we who brought the tropics to the island. When I knew the town, it didn't end in sandy beaches and coconut trees, but in a tainted swamp, in mangrove and mud. Then the land was reclaimed from the sea, and the people who got oysters from the mangrove disappeared. On the reclaimed land we built the tropics. We put up our army huts, raised our flag, planted our coconut trees and our hedges. Among the great wooden buildings with wire-netting windows we scattered pretty little thatched huts.

We brought the tropics to the island. Yet to the islanders it must have seemed that we had brought America to them. Everyone worked for us. You asked a man what he did; he didn't say that he drove a truck or was a carpenter; he simply said he worked for the Americans. Every morning trucks drove through the city, picking up workers; and every afternoon the trucks left the base to take them back.

The islanders came to our bit of the tropics. We explored theirs. Nothing was organized in those days. There were no leaflets telling you where to shop or where to go. You had to find out yourself. You found out quickly about the bars; it wasn't pleasant to be beaten up or robbed.

I heard about Henry's place from a man on the base. He said Henry kept a few goats in his backyard and sometimes slaughtered them on a Sunday. He said Henry was a character. It didn't seem a particularly enticing thing. But I got into a taxi outside the base one Thursday afternoon and decided to look. Taxi drivers know everything; so they say.

'Do you know a man called Henry?' I asked the taxi driver. 'He keeps a few goats.'

'The island small, boss, but not that small.'

'You must know him. He keeps these goats.'

'No, boss, you be frank with me, I be frank with you. If goats you after. . . .'

I allowed him to take me where he wished. We drove through the old ramshackle city, wooden houses on separate lots, all decay, it seemed, in the middle of the brightest vegetation. It scarcely seemed a city where you would, by choice, seek pleasure; it made you think only of empty afternoons. All these streets looked so quiet and alike. All the houses looked so tame and dull and alike: very little people attending to their very little affairs.

The taxi driver took me to various rooms, curtained, hot, stuffed with furniture, and squalid enough to kill all thoughts of pleasure. In one room there was even a baby. 'Not mine, not mine,' the girl said. I was a little strained, and the driver was strained, by the time we came to the street where he said I would find Henry's place.

The brave young man looking for fun. The spark had gone; and to tell the truth, I was a little embarrassed. I wished to arrive at Henry's alone. I paid the taxi driver off.

I imagine I was hoping to find something which at least looked like a commercial establishment. I looked for boards and signs. I saw nothing. I walked past shuttered houses to a shuttered grocery, the only clue even there being a small black noticeboard saying, in amateurish letters, that Ma-Ho was licensed to deal in spirituous liquors. I walked down the other side of the street. And here was something I had missed. Outside a house much hung with ferns a board said:

Premier Commercial College
Shorthand and Bookkeeping
H. J. Blackwhite, Principal

Here and there a curtain flapped. My walks up and down the short street had begun to attract attention. Too late to give up, though. I walked back past the Premier Commercial College. This time a boy was hanging out of a window. He was wearing a tie and he was giggling.

I asked him, 'Hey, does your sister screw?'

The boy opened his mouth and wailed and pulled back his head. There were giggles from behind the ferns. A tall man pushed open a door with coloured glass panes and came out to the veranda. He looked sombre. He wore black trousers, a white shirt, and a black tie. He had a rod in his hand!

He said in an English accent, 'Will you take your filth elsewhere. This is a school. We devote ourselves to things of the mind.' He pointed sternly to the board.

'Sorry, Mr – '

He pointed to the board again. 'Blackwhite. Mr H. J.

Blackwhite. My patience is at an end. I shall sit down and type out a letter of protest to the newspapers.'

'I feel like writing some sort of protest myself. Do you know a place called Henry's?'

'This is not Henry's.'

'Sorry, sorry. But before you go away, tell me, what do you people do?'

'What do you mean, do?'

'What do you people do when you are doing nothing? Why do you keep on?'

There were more giggles behind the ferns. Mr Blackwhite turned and ran through the coloured glass doors into the drawingroom. I heard him beating on a desk with a rod and shouting: 'Silence, silence.' In the silence which he instantly obtained he beat a boy. Then he reappeared on the veranda, his sleeves rolled up, his face shining with sweat. He seemed willing enough to keep on exchanging words with me, but just then some army jeeps turned the corner and we heard men and women shouting. Overdoing the gaiety, I thought. Blackwhite's look of exaltation was replaced by one of distaste and alarm.

'Your colleagues and companions,' he said.

He disappeared, with a sort of controlled speed, behind the glass panes. His class began to sing, 'Flow gently, sweet Afton.'

The jeeps stopped at the unfenced lot opposite Mr Blackwhite's. This lot contained two verandaless wooden houses. Small houses on low concrete pillars; possibly there were more houses at the back. I stood on the pavement, the jeep-loads tumbled out. I half hoped that the gay tide would sweep me in. But men and girls just passed on either side of me, and when the tide had washed into the houses and the yard I remained where I was, stranded on the pavement.

Henry's, it was clear, was like a club. Everybody seemed to know everybody else and was making a big thing of it. I stood around. No one took any notice of me. I tried to give the impression that I was waiting for someone. I felt very foolish. Pleasure was soon the last thing in my mind. Dignity became much more important.

Henry's was especially difficult because it appeared to have no commercial organization. There was no bar, there were no waiters. The gay crowd simply sat around on the flights of concrete steps that led from the rocky ground to the doors. No tables outside, and no chairs. I could see things like this inside some of the rooms, but I wasn't sure whether I had the right to go into any of them. It was clearly a place to which you couldn't come alone.

It was Henry in the end who spoke to me. He said that I was making him nervous and that I was making the girls nervous. The girls were like racehorses, he said, very nervous and sensitive. Then, as though explaining everything, he said, 'The place is what you see it is.'

'It's very nice,' I said.

'You don't have to flatter me; if you want to stay here, fine; if you don't want to stay here, that's fine too.'

Henry wasn't yet a character. He was still only working up to it. I don't like characters. They worry me, and perhaps it was because Henry wasn't yet a character – a public performer, jolly but excluding – that I fell in so easily with him. Later, when he became a character, I was one of the characters with him; it was we that did the excluding.

I clung to him that first afternoon for the sake of dignity, as I say. Also, I felt a little resentful of the others, so very gay and integrated, and did not wish to be alone.

'We went out,' Henry said. 'A little excursion, you know. That bay over the hills, the only one you people leave us. I don't know, you people say you come here to fight a war, and the first thing you do you take away our beaches. You take all the white sand beaches; you leave us only black sand.'

'You know these bureaucrats. They like things tidy.'

'I know,' he said. 'They like it tidy here too. I can't tell you the number of people who would like to run me out of town.'

'Like that man across the road?'

'Oh, you meet old Blackwhite?'

'He is going to type out a letter about me to the newspapers. And about you, too, I imagine. And your colleagues
and companions.'

'They don't print all Blackwhite's letters. Good relations
and all that, you know. He believe he stand a better chance
with the typewriter. Tell me what you do to provoke him.
I never see a man look as quiet as you.'

'I asked one of his boys whether he had a sister who screwed.'

Amusement went strangely on Henry's sour face. He
looked the ascetic sort. His hair was combed straight back
and his narrow-waisted trousers were belted with a tie. This
was the one raffish, startling thing about his dress.

Henry went on: 'The trouble with the natives – '

I started at the word.

'Yes, natives. The troubles with the natives is that they
don't like me. I don't belong here, you know. I am like you.
I come from another place. A pretty little island, if I tell you.
I build up all this from scratch.' He waved at his yard. 'These
people here lazy and they damn jealous with it too. They
always trying to get me deported. Illegal immigrant and so
on. But they can't touch me. I have all the shots in the palm
of my hand. You hear people talk about Gordon? Black
man; but the best lawyer we have. Gordon was always
coming here until that divorce business. Big thing. You
probably hear about that on the base.'

'Sure, we heard about it.'

'And whenever I have any little trouble about this illegal
immigrant business, I just go straight, like man, to Gordon
office. The clerks – you know, those fellows with ties – try
to be rude, and I just telling them, "You tell Alfred" – his
name is Alfred Gordon – "you tell Alfred that Henry here."
And everybody falling back in amazement when Mr Gordon
come out heself and shaking me by the hand and muching me
up in front of everybody. "All you wait," he say, "I got to
see my old friend Henry." And teeth.'

'Teeth?'

'Teeth. Whenever I want to have any teeth pull out, I just run up to old Ling-Wing – Chinee, but the best dentist we have in the place – and he pulling out the teeth straight way. You got to have a philosophy of life. Look, I go tell you,' he said, 'my father was a good-for-nothing. Always gambling, a game called wappee and all-fours. And whenever my mother complain and start bawling out, "Hezekiah, what you going to leave for your children?" my father he only saying, "I ain't got land. I ain't got money. But I going to leave my children a wonderful set of friends." '

'That's a fine philosophy,' I said.

'We all have to corporate in some way. Some people corporate in one way, some corporate another way. I think that you and me going to get on good. Mavis, pour this man a drink. He is a wonderful talker.'

Henry, sipping at rum-and-cokes all the time, was maudlin. I was a little high myself.

One of the Americans who had been on the excursion to the bay came up to us. He tottered a little. He said he had to leave.

'I know,' Henry said. 'The war etcetera.'

'How much do I owe you, Henry?'

'You know what you owe me. I don't keep no check.'

'Let me see. I think I had a chicken pilau. Three or four rum-and-cokes.'

'Good,' Henry said. 'You just pay for that.'

The man paid. Henry took his money without any comment. When the man left he said, 'Drink is never any excuse. I don't believe people ever not knowing what they do. He not coming back in here. He had two chicken pilaus, six rum-and-coke, five bottles soda water and two whiskies. That's what I call vice.'

'It is vice, and I am ashamed of him.'

'I will tell you, you know,' Henry said. 'When the old queen pass on – '

'The old queen?'

'My mother. I was in a sort of daze. Then I had this little dream. The old man, he appear to me.'

'Your father Hezekiah?'

'No. God. He say, "Henry, surround yourself with love, but avoid vice." On this island I was telling you about, pretty if I tell you, they had this woman, pretty but malevolent. She make two-three children for me, and bam, you know what, she want to rush me into marriage.'

The sun was going down. From the base, the bit of the tropics we had created, the bugle sounded Retreat. Henry snapped his fingers, urging us all to stand. We stood up and saluted to the end.

'I like these little customs,' he said. 'Is a nice little custom you boys bring with you.'

'About this woman on the pretty island with two or three children?'

Henry said, 'I avoided vice. I ran like hell. I get the rumour spread that I dead. I suppose I am dead in a way. Can't go back to my pretty little island. Oh, prettier than this. Pretty, pretty. But she waiting for me.'

We heard hymns from the street.

'Money,' Henry said, 'all you girls got your money ready?'

They all got out little coins and we went out to the pavement. A tall bearded man, white-robed and sandalled, was leading a little group of hymn-singers, six small black girls in white gowns. They were sweet hymns; we listened in silence.

Then the bearded man said, 'Brothers and sisters, it is customary on such occasions to say that there is still time to repent.' He was like a man in love with his own fluency. His accent was very English. 'It is, however, my belief that this, at this time, is one of the optimistic assertions of fraudulent evangelists more concerned with the counting of money than what I might call the count-down of our imminent destruction.' Suddenly his manner changed. He paused, closed his eyes, swayed a little, lifted up his arms and shouted, in an entirely different voice: 'The word of the Bible is coming to pass.'

Some of Henry's girls chanted back: 'What word?' And others, 'What part?'

The white-robed man said, 'The part where it say young people going to behave bad, and evil and violence going to stalk the land. That part.'

His little chorus began to sing; and he went around collecting from us, saying, 'It is nothing personal, you understand, nothing personal. I know you boys have to be here defending us and so on, but the truth is the truth.'

He collected his money, slipped it into a pocket of his robe, patted the pocket; then he seemed to go on patting. He patted each of his singers, either out of a great love, or to make sure that they had not hidden any of the coins they had received. Then: 'Right-wheel!' he called above their singing; and, patting them on the shoulder as they passed him, followed them to the grocery at the corner. His hymn meeting continued there, under the rusty corrugated-iron eaves.

It was now dark. A picnic atmosphere came to Henry's yard. Meals were being prepared in various rooms; gramophones were playing. From distant yards came the sound of steel-bands. Night provided shelter, and in the yard it was very cosy, very like a family gathering. Only, I was not yet of the family.

A girl with a sling bag came in. She greeted Henry, and he greeted her with a largeness of gesture which yet concealed a little reserve, a little awe. He called her Selma. I noted her. I became the third in the party; I became nervous.

I am always nervous in the presence of beauty; and in such a setting, faced with a person I couldn't assess, I was a little frightened. I didn't know the rules of Henry's place and it was clear that the place had its own rules. I was inexperienced. Inexperienced, I say. Yet what good has experience brought me since? I still, in such a situation and in such a place, move between the extremes of courtesy and loudness.

Selma was unattached and cool. I thought she had the

coolness that comes either from ownership or from being owned. It was this as much as dress and manner and balance which marked her out from the others in the yard. She might have been Henry's girl, the replacement for that other, abandoned on the pretty little island; or she might have belonged to someone who had not yet appeared.

The very private greetings over, Henry introduced us.

'He's quite a talker,' he said.

'He's a good listener,' I said.

She asked Henry, 'Did he hear Priest talk?'

I answered, 'I did. That was some sermon.'

'I always like hearing a man use language well,' she said.

'He certainly does,' I said.

'You can see,' she said, 'that he's an educated man.'

'You could see that.'

There was a pause. 'He sells insurance,' she said, 'when he's not preaching.'

'It sounds a wonderful combination. He frightens us about death, and then sells us insurance.'

She wasn't amused. 'I would like to be insured.'

'You are far too young.'

'But that is just the time. The terms are better. I don't know, I would just like it. I feel it's nice. I have an aunt in the country. She is always making old style because she's insured. Whenever she buys a little more she always lets you know.'

'Well, why don't you buy some insurance yourself?'

She said, 'I am very poor.'

And she said the words in such a way that it seemed to put a fullstop to our conversation. I hate the poor and the humble. I think poverty is something we should all conceal. Selma spoke of it as something she was neither proud nor ashamed of; it was a condition which was soon to be changed. Little things like this occur in all relationships, little warning abrasions in the smoothness of early intercourse which we choose to ignore. We always deceive ourselves; we cannot say we have not been warned.

'What would you do if you had a lot of money?'

'I would buy lots of things,' she said after some thought. 'Lots of nice modern things.'

'What sort of things?'

'A three-piece suite. One of those deep ones. You sink into them. I'd buy a nice counterpane, satiny and thick and crisscrossed with deep lines. I saw Norma Shearer using one in *Escape*.'

'A strange thing. That's all I remember of that picture. What do you think she was doing in that bed then? But that was an eiderdown she had, you know. You don't need an eiderdown in this part of the world. It's too warm.'

'Well, whatever you call it, I'd like that. And shoes, I'd buy lots of shoes. Do you have nightmares?'

'Always.'

'You know mine?'

'Tell me.'

'I am in town, you know. Walking down Regent Street. People staring at me, and I feel: this is new. I don't feel embarrassed. I feel like a beauty queen. Then I see myself in a shop window. I am barefoot. I always wake up then. My feet are hanging over the bed.'

I was still nervous. The conversation always seemed to turn away from the point to which I felt I ought to bring it, though to tell the truth I had lost the wish to do so. Still, we owe a duty to ourselves.

I said, 'Do you come from the city?'

'I come from the country.'

Question, answer, fullstop. I tried again. Henry was near us, a bottle in his hand.

I said, 'What makes a girl like you come to a place like this?' And, really, I was ashamed of the words almost before I said them.

'That's what I call a vicious question,' Henry said.

At the same time Selma slapped me.

'You think that's a nice question?' Henry said. 'I think that's a vicious question. I think that's obscene.' He pointed through the open doorway to a little sign in one of the inner rooms: Be obscene but not heard. 'It's not something we talk about.'

'I am sorry.'

'It's not for me that I am worried,' he said. 'It's for Selma. I don't know, but that girl always bringing out the vice in people. She bring out the vice in Blackwhite across the road. Don't say anything, but I see it in his eye: he want to reform her. And you know what reform is? Reform mean: keep off, for me alone. She bring out the vice in Priest. He don't want to reform. He just want. Look, Frankie, one set of people come here and then too another set come here. Selma is a educated girl, you know. Cambridge Junior Certificate. Latin and French and geometry and all that sort of thing. She does work in one of the big stores. Not one of those little Syrian shops, you know. She come here every now and then, you come here. That is life. Let us leave the vice outside, let us leave the vice outside. A lot of these girls work in stores. Any time I want a shirt, I just pass around these stores, and these girls give me shirts. We have to help one another.'

I said, 'You must have a lot of shirts.'

'Yes, I have a lot of shirts. Look, I will tell you. Selma and one or two of the other people you see here, we call *wabeen*.'

'Wabeen?'

'One of our freshwater fish. A lil loose. A *lil*. Not for any and everybody. You understand? Wabeen is not *spote*.'

'Spote?'

'Spote is – don't make me use obscene language, man, Frank. Spote is what you see.' He waved his hands about the yard.

The steel-bands sounded nearer, and then through a gate in the corrugated iron fence at the back of the lot the musicians came in. Their instruments were made out of old dustbins, and on these instruments they played a coarse music I had never heard before.

'They have to hide, you know,' Henry told me. 'It's illegal. The war and so on. Helping the war effort.'

There was a little open shed at the back. It had a black-board. I had noticed that blackboard and wondered about it. In this shed two or three people now began to dance. They drew watchers to them; they converted watchers into parti-cipants. From rooms in the houses on Henry's lot, from rooms in other back-yards, and from the sewerage trace at the back, people drifted in steadily to watch. Each dancer was on his own. Each dancer lived with a private frenzy. Women among the watchers tore twigs from the hibiscus hedges and from time to time, as though offering benediction and reward, beat the dancers' dusty feet with green leaves.

Henry put his arm over my shoulder and led me to where Selma was standing. He kept one hand on my shoulder; he put the other on her shoulder. We stood silently together, watching. His hands healed us, bound us.

A whistle blew. There were cries of 'Police!' and in an instant the yard was transformed. Dustbins appeared upright here and there; liquor bottles disappeared inside some; the dancers and the audience sat in neat rows under the shed and one man stood at the blackboard, writing. Many of Henry's girls put on spectacles. One or two carried pieces of em-broidery.

It seemed to me that the police were a long time in enter-ing. When they did, the Inspector shook Henry by the hand and said, 'The old Adult Education class, eh?'

'As you see,' Henry said. 'Each one teach one.'

The Inspector closed his fingers when he took away his hand from Henry's. He became chatty. 'I don't know, boy,' he said. 'We just have to do this. Old Blackwhite really on your tail. And that Mrs Lambert, she too lodge a complaint.'

I wonder, though, whether I would have become involved with Selma and the others, if, during that first evening after I had undressed and was lying with Selma, I hadn't seen my clothes dancing out of the window. They danced; it was as though they had taken on a life of their own.

I called out to Selma.

She didn't seem surprised. She said, 'I think they are fishing tonight.'

'Fishing?' I ran to the window after my disappearing clothes.

'Yes, you know, fishing through the windows. Lifting a shirt here, a pair of trousers there. It is no good chasing them. Carnival coming, you know, and everybody wants a pretty costume.'

She was right. In the morning I woke up and remembered that I had no clothes except for my pants and vest. I threw open the back window and saw naked Americans hanging out of windows. We looked at one another. We exchanged no words. The evening was past; this was the morning.

Boys and girls were going into Mr Blackwhite's college. Some stopped to examine contraceptives thrown into the gutters. Selma herself was fully dressed when I saw her. She said she was going to work. So it seemed after all that Henry's story about some of his girls working in stores was right. Henry himself brought me a cup of coffee.

'You can have one of my shirts. I just pass around and ask them for one, you know.'

The morning life of Henry's yard was different from the evening life. There was a subdued workaday bustle everywhere. A tall thin man was doing limbering-up exercises. He wore a vest and a pair of shorts, and from time to time he rubbed himself with oil from a little phial.

'Canadian Healing Oil,' Henry said. 'I like to give him a little encouragement. Mano is a walker, you know. But a little too impatient; he does always end up by running and getting disqualified.'

'This is terrible,' I said. 'But what about my clothes?'

'You've got to learn tolerance. This is the one thing you have got to learn on the island.'

Mano was squatting and springing up. All about him coalpots were being fanned on back steps and women were preparing morning meals. A lot of green everywhere, more than I had remembered. Beyond the sewerage trace I could see the equally forested back-yards of the houses of the other street, and it was in some of these yards that I saw khaki uniforms and white sailor uniforms hanging limp from lines.

Henry followed my eyes. 'Carnival coming, Frank. And you people got the whole world. Some people corporate in one way, some in another.'

I didn't want Henry's philosophy just then. I ran out as I was on to the pavement. By the standards of the street I wasn't too badly dressed in my vest and pants. Next door an old negro sat sunning himself in the doorway of a room which looked like a declining secondhand bookshop. He was dressed in a tight-fitting khaki suit. The open door carried on its inside a flowery sign – MR W. LAMBERT, BOOKBINDER – so that I understood how, with the front door closed, the house was the respectable shuttered residence I had seen the day before, and how now, with the front door open, it was a shop. Beside Mr Lambert – I thought it safe to assume that he was Mr Lambert – was a small glass of rum. As I passed him he lifted the glass against the light, squinted at it, nodded to me and said, 'Good morning, my Yankee friend, may God all blessings to you send.' Then he drank the rum at a gulp and the look of delight on his face was replaced by one of total torment, as though the rum and the morning greeting formed part of an obnoxious daily penance.

'Good morning.'

'If it is not being rude, tell me, my good sir, why you are nude.'

'I don't have any clothes.'

'Touché, I say. Naked we come, and naked go away.'

This was interesting and worth exploring but just then at the end of the road I saw the jeep. I didn't know what the punishment was for losing your uniform and appearing naked in public. I ran back past Mr Lambert. He looked a little startled, like a man seeing visions. I ran into the side of Henry's yard and went up to the front house by the back steps. At the same time Mano, the walker, began walking briskly out from the other side of the house into the road.

I heard someone say from the jeep, 'Doesn't it look to you that he went in white and came out black?'

A window opened in the next room and an American voice called out, 'Did you see a naked white man running down here this morning, a few minutes ago?'

A woman's voice said, 'Look, mister, the morning is my period of rest, and the last thing I want to see in the morning is a prick.'

A pause, and the SPs drove off.

For me there remained the problem of clothing. Henry offered to lend me some of his. They didn't exactly fit. 'But,' he said, 'you could pass around by Selma's store and get a shirt. Look, I'll give you the address.'

A bicycle bell rang from the road. It was the postman in his uniform.

'Henry, Henry,' he said. 'Look what I bringing today.'

He came inside and showed a parcel. It was for Mr Blackwhite and had been sent to him from a publisher in the United States.

'Another one come back, another one.'

'O my God!' Henry said. 'I'm going to have Blackwhite crying on my hands again. What was this one about?'

'Usual thing,' the postman said. 'Love. I had a good little read. In fact, it was funny in parts.' He pulled out the manuscript. 'You want to hear?'

Henry looked at me.

'I am a captive audience,' I said.

'Make yourself comfortable,' the postman said. He began to read: '"Lady Theresa Phillips was the most sought-after girl in all the county of Shropshire. Beautiful, an heiress to boot, intelligent, well-versed in the classics, skilful in repartee and with the embroidery needle, superbly endowed in short, she had but one failing, that of pride. She spurned all who wooed her. She had sent frustrated lovers to Italy, to the distant colonies, there to pine away in energetic solitude. Yet Nemesis was at hand. At a ball given by Lord Severn, the noblest lord in the land, Lady Theresa met Lord Alistair

Grant. He was tall, square-shouldered and handsome, with melancholy eyes that spoke of deep suffering; he had in fact been left an orphan." '

'Christ! Is this what he always writes about?'

'All the time,' Henry said. 'Only lords and ladies. Typing like a madman all day. And Sundays especially you hear that machine going.'

The front door was open and through it now came the voice of Mr Blackwhite. 'Henry, I have seen everything this morning, and Mrs Lambert has just been to see me. I shall be typing out a letter to the newspapers. I just can't have naked men running about my street.' He caught sight of the postman and caught sight of the manuscript in the postman's hand. His face fell. He raced up the concrete steps into the room and snatched the manuscript away. 'Albert, I've told you before. You must stop this tampering with His Majesty's mail. It is the sort of thing they chop off your head for.'

'They send it back, old man,' Henry said. 'If you ask me, Blackwhite, I think it's just a case of prejudice. Open-and-shut case. I sit down quiet-quiet and listen to what Albert read out, and it was really nice. It was really nice.'

Blackwhite softened. 'You really think so, Henry?'

'Yes, man, it was really nice. I can't wait to hear what happen to Lady Theresa Phillips.'

'No. You are lying, you are lying.'

'What happened in the end, Mr Blackwhite?' I slapped at an ant on my leg.

'You just scratch yourself and keep quiet,' he said to me. 'I hate you. I don't believe you can even read. You think that black people don't write, eh?'

Albert the postman said, 'It was a real nice story, Black-white. And I prophesy, boy, that one day all those white people who now sending back your books going to be coming here and begging you to write for them.'

'Let them beg, let them beg. I won't write for them when they beg. Oh, my God. All that worrying, all that typing.

Not going to write a single line more. Not a blasted line.'
He grew wild again. 'I hate you, Henry, too. I am going to
have this place closed, if it's the last thing I do.'

Henry threw up his hands.

'To hell with you,' Blackwhite said. 'To hell with Lady
Theresa Phillips.' To me he said, pointing, 'You don't like
me.' And then to Henry: 'And you don't like me either.
Henry, I don't know how a man could change like you. At
one time it was always Niya Binghi and death to the whites.
Now you could just wrap yourself in the Stars and Stripes
and parade the streets.'

'Niya Binghi?' I asked.

'Was during the Abyssinian War,' Henry said, 'and the
old queen did just die. Death to the whites. Twenty million
on the march. You know our black people. The great revenge. Twenty million on the march. And always when you
look back, is you alone. Nobody behind you. But the Stars
and Stripes,' he added. 'You know, Blackwhite, I believe you
have an idea there. Good idea for Carnival. Me as sort of
Uncle Sam. Gentleman, it have such a thing as Stars and
Stripes at the base?'

'Oh, he's one of those, is he?' Blackwhite said. 'One of our
American merchantmen?'

'I believe I can get you a Stars and Stripes,' I said.

Blackwhite went silent. I could see he was intrigued. His
aggressiveness when he spoke wasn't very convincing. 'I
suppose that you people have the biggest typewriters in the
world, as you have the biggest everything else?'

'It's too early in the morning for obscene language,'
Henry said.

'I am not boasting,' I said. 'But I am always interested in
writing and writers. Tell me, Mr Blackwhite, do you work
regularly, or do you wait for inspiration?'

The question pleased him. He said, 'It is a mixture of
both, a mixture of both.'

'Do you write it out all in longhand, or do you use a typewriter?'

'On the typewriter. But I am not being bribed, remember. I am not being bribed. But if the naked gentleman is interested in our native customs and local festivals, I am prepared to listen.' His manner changed. 'Tell me, man, you have a little pattern book of uniforms? I don't want to appear in any and every sort of costume at Carnival, you know.'

'Some of those costumes can be expensive,' I said.

'Money, money,' Blackwhite said. 'It had to come up. But of course I will pay.'

This was how it started; this was how I began to be a purveyor of naval supplies. First to Mr Henry and to Mr Blackwhite and then to the street. I brought uniforms; money changed hands. I brought steel drums; money changed hands. I brought cartons of cigarettes and chewing gum; money changed hands. I brought a couple of Underwood standard typewriters. Money didn't change hands.

Blackwhite said, 'Frankie, I think art ought to be its own reward.'

It wasn't though. A new line went up on Blackwhite's board:

ALSO TYPING LESSONS

'Also typing lessons, Blackwhite?'

'Also typing lessons. Black people don't type?'

This had become his joke. We were in his room. His walls were hung with coloured drawings of the English countryside in spring. There were many of these, but they were not as numerous as the photographs of himself, in black and white, in sepia, in coarse colour. He had an especially large photograph of himself between smaller ones of Churchill and Roosevelt.

'The trouble, you know, Blackwhite,' I said, 'is that you are not black at all.'

'What do you mean?'

'You are terribly white.'

'God, I am not going to be insulted by a beachcomber.'

'Beachcomber. That's very good. But you are not only

white. You are English. All those lords and ladies, Blackwhite. All that Jane Austen.'

'What's wrong with that? Why should I deny myself any aspect of the world?'

'Rubbish. I was wondering, though, whether you couldn't start writing about the island. Writing about Selma and Mano and Henry and the others.'

'But you think they will want to read about these people? These people don't exist, you know. This is just an interlude for you, Frankie. This is your little Greenwich Village. I know, I can read. Bam bam, bram, bram. Fun. Afterwards you leave us and go back. This place, I tell you, is nowhere. It doesn't exist. People are just born here. They all want to go away, and for you it is only a holiday. I don't want to be any part of your Greenwich Village. You beachcomb, you buy sympathy. The big rich man always behind the love, the I-am-just-like-you. I have been listening to you talking to people in Henry's yard about the States; about the big cinemas with wide screens and refrigerators as big as houses and everybody becoming film stars and presidents. And you are damn frightened of the whole thing. Always ready for the injection of rum, always looking for the nice and simple natives to pick you up.'

It was so. We turn experience continually into stories to lend drama to dullness, to maintain our self-respect. But we never see ourselves; only occasionally do we get an undistorted reflection. He was right. I was buying sympathy, I was buying fellowship. And I knew, better than he had said, the fraudulence of my position in the street.

He pointed to Churchill on the wall. 'What do you think would have happened to him if he was born here?'

'Hold your head that way, Blackwhite. Yes, definitely Churchillian.'

'Funny. You think we would have been hearing about him today? He would have been working in a bank. He would have been in the civil service. He would have been importing sewing machines and exporting cocoa.'

I studied the photograph.

'You like this street. You like those boys in the back-yard beating the pans. You like Selma who has nowhere to go, poor little wabeen. Big thing, big love. But she is only a wabeen and you are going back, and neither of you is fooling the other. You like Mr Lambert sitting on the steps drinking his one glass of rum in the morning and tacking up a few ledgers. Because Mr Lambert can only drink one glass of rum in the morning and tack up a few ledgers. You like seeing Mano practising for the walking race that is never going to come off. You look at these things and you say, "How nice, how quaint, this is what life should be." You don't see that we here are all mad and we are getting madder all the time, turning life into a Carnival.'

And Carnival came.

It had been permitted that year under stringent police supervision. The men from the yards near Henry's made up their bands in the uniforms I had provided; and paraded through the streets. Henry was Uncle Sam; Selma was the Empress Theodora; the other girls were slave girls and concubines. There were marines and infantrymen and airforce pilots fighting on the Pacific atolls; and in a jeep with which I had provided him stood Mr Blackwhite. He stood still, dressed in a fantastically braided uniform. He wore dark glasses, smoked a corn-cob pipe and his left hand was held aloft in a salute which was like a benediction. He did not dance, he did not sway to the music. He was MacArthur, promising to return.

On the Tuesday evening, when the streets were full of great figures – Napoleon, Julius Caesar, Richard the Lionheart: men parading with concentration – Blackwhite was also abroad, dressed like Shakespeare.

Selma and I settled down into a relationship which was only occasionally stormy. I had taken Mr Henry's advice that first morning and had gone around to the store where she worked. She did not acknowledge me. My rough clothes, which were really Henry's, attracted a good deal of critical attention and much critical comment on the behaviour of Americans. She acknowledged me later: she was pleased that I had gone to see her in a period as cool and disenchanted as the morning after.

Henry's, as I said, seemed to have its own especial rules. It was a club, a meeting-place, a haven, a place of assignation. It attracted all sorts. Selma belonged to that type of island girl who moved from relationship to relationship, from man to man. She feared marriage because marriage, for a girl of the people, was full of perils and quick degradation. She felt that once she surrendered completely to any one man, she lost her hold on him, and her beauty was useless, a wasted gift.

She said, 'Sometimes when I am walking I look at these *warrahoons*, and I think that for some little girl somewhere this animal is lord and master. *He. He* doesn't like corn-flakes. *He* doesn't like rum. *He* this, *he* that.'

Her job in the store and Henry's protection gave her independence. She did not wish to lose this; she never fell for glamour. She was full of tales of girls she had known who had broken the code of their group and actually married visitors; and then had led dreadful lives, denied both the freedom they had had and the respectability, the freedom from struggle, which marriage ought to have brought.

So we settled down, after making a little pact.

'Remember,' she said, 'you are free and I am free. I am free to do exactly what I want, and you are free too.'

The pressing had always been mine. It wasn't an easy pact. I knew that this freedom might at any time embrace either Blackwhite, shy reformer in the background, or the white-robed preacher whom we called Priest. They both continued to make their interest in her plain.

But in the beginning it was not from these men that we found opposition after we had settled down in one of the smaller jalousied houses in the street – and in those days it was possible to buy a house for fifteen hundred dollars. No, it was not from these men that there was opposition, but from Mrs Lambert, Henry's neighbour, the wife of the man in the khaki suit who sipped the glass of rum in the mornings and spoke in rhyme to express either delight or pain.

Now Mrs Lambert was a surprise. I had seen her in the street for some time without connecting her with Mr Lambert. Mr Lambert was black and Mrs Lambert was white. She was about fifty and she had the manners of the street. It was my own fault, in a way, that I had attracted her hostility. I had put money in the Lamberts' way and had given them, too late in life, a position to keep up or to lose.

Mr Lambert had been excited by the boom conditions that had begun to prevail in the street. The words were Ma-Ho's, he who ran the grocery at the corner. Ma-Ho had begun to alter and extend his establishment to include a café where many men from the base and many locals sat on high stools and ate hot dogs and drank Coca-Colas, and where the children from several streets around congregated, waiting to be treated.

'Offhand,' Ma-Ho said, for he was fond of talking, 'I would say, boom.' And the words 'offhand' and 'boom' were the only really distinct ones. He began every sentence with 'offhand'; what followed was very hard to understand. Yet he was always engaged in conversation with some captive customer.

The walls of his grocery carried pictures of Chiang Kai-shek and Madame Chiang. They also had pictorial calendars, several years out of date, with delicately tinted Chinese beauties languid or coy against a background of ordered rocks and cultivated weeds, picturesque birds and waterfalls which poured like oil: incongruous in the shop with its chipped grimy counter, its open sacks of flour, its khaki-coloured sacks of sugar, its open tins of red, liquid butter. These pictures were like a longing for another world; and indeed, Ma-Ho did not plan to stay on the island. When you asked him, making conversation, especially on those occasions when you were short of change and wanted a little trust from him, 'You still going back?' the answer was: 'Offhand, I say two-four years.'

His children remained distinctive, and separate from the life of the street: a small neat crocodile, each child armed with neat bags and neat pencil boxes, going coolly off to school in the morning and returning just as coolly in the afternoon, as though nothing had touched them during the whole day, or caused them to be sullied. In the morning the back door of his shop opened to let out these children; in the afternoon the back door opened to swallow them in again; and nothing more was heard from them, and nothing more was seen of them.

The boom touched Ma-Ho. It touched Mrs Lambert. Mr Lambert called very formally one evening in his khaki suit and put a proposal to me.

'I don't want to see you get into trouble,' he said. 'Mrs Lambert and I have been talking things over, and we feel you are running an unnecessary risk in bringing these – what should I say? – these supplies to the needy of our poor island.'

I said, 'It's worked quite all right so far. You should see all the stuff we throw away.'

'Now don't misunderstand,' he said. 'I am not blaming you for what you are doing. But Mrs Lambert is particularly concerned about the trucks. She feels that by having them come out with these supplies and then having them go back, there is a chance of them being checked twice.'

'I see what you mean. Thanks, Mr Lambert. You mean that Mrs Lambert thinks that perhaps a truck might just slip out of the base and stay out?'

'Mrs Lambert thought it might be safer. Mrs Lambert has a relation who knows all there is to be known about trucks and motor vehicles generally.'

I said nothing just then, thinking of the possibilities.

Mr Lambert's manner broke up. It became familiar. All the people in the street had two sets of manners, one extremely formal, one rallying and casual.

'Look,' Mr Lambert said. 'The truck go back to the base, they start one set of questioning. It stay out here, ten to one they forget all about it. You people own the whole world.'

So into Mr Lambert's yard a truck one day rolled; and when, a fortnight or so later, it rolled out again, it was scarcely recognizable.

'Lend-lease, lease-lend,' Mr Lambert said with pure delight. 'The trend, my friend.'

And it was this truck that the Lamberts hired out to the contractors on the base. The contractors provided a driver and were willing – in fact, anxious – for the truck to work two shifts a day.

'We are getting twenty dollars a day,' Mr Lambert said. 'My friend, what luck! What luck you've given with a simple truck!'

Part of this luck, needless to say, I shared.

Yet all this while Mrs Lambert remained in the background. She was a figure in a curtained window; she was someone walking briskly down the street. She was never someone you exchanged words with. She never became part of the life of the street.

'That is one person whose old age you spoil,' Henry said. 'You see? She behaving as though they *buy* that truck. I don't think this is going to end good.'

Twenty dollars a day, minus commission and gasoline. The money was piling up; and then one day we saw a whole group of workmen around the Lamberts' house, like ants around a dead cockroach. The street came out to watch. The house, small and wooden, was lifted off its pillars by the workmen. The front door with the sign 'Mr W Lambert, Bookbinder' swung open and kept on flapping while the house was taken to the back of the lot, to rest not on pillars but flat on the ground. The workmen drank glasses of rum to celebrate. The street cheered. But then we saw Mr Lambert pushing his way through the crowd. He looked like a man expecting news of death. He saw the pillars; he saw his house on the ground; and he said: 'My house! My house brought low! But I did not want a bungalow. Here the old pillars stand, in the middle of naked land.' He left and went to Ma-Ho's. He became drunk; he addressed verse to everyone. The habit grew on him. It seemed to us that he remained drunk until he died.

Henry said, 'Once upon a time – and really now it sounded like a fairy tale – once upon a time Mrs Lambert was a very poor girl. Family from Corsica. Living up there in the cocoa valleys with the tall *immortelle* trees. Times was hard. You couldn't even give away cocoa. And Lambert had this job in the Civil Service. Messenger. Uniform, regular pay, the old pension at the end, and nobody sacking you. Marriage up there in the hills with the bush and red *immortelle* flowers. Oh, happy! Once-upon-a-time fairy tale. Wur-thering Heights. Hansel and Gretel in the witch-broom cocoa woods. Then the world sort of catch up with them.'

The pillars were knocked down, and where the old wooden house stood there presently began to rise a house of patterned concrete blocks. The house, I could see, was going to be like hundreds of others in the city: three bedrooms down one side, a veranda, drawingroom and diningroom down the other side, and a back veranda.

No longer a doorstep at which Mr Lambert could sit, greeting us in the morning with his glass of rum. The old wooden house was sold, for the materials; frame by frame, jalousie by jalousie, the house was dismantled and re-erected far away by the man who had bought it, somewhere in the country. And then there was no longer a Mr Lambert in the morning. He left the yard early. In his khaki suit he was like a workman hurrying off to a full day. We often saw him walking with Mano. Mano, the walker in Henry's yard, who after his morning's exercise put on his khaki messenger's uniform and walked to the government office where he worked. Their dress was alike, but they were an ill-assorted pair, Mano lean and athletic, Mr Lambert even at that early hour shambling drunk.

Mr Lambert had a sideline. At sports meetings, on race days, at cricket and football matches, he ran a stall. He sold a vile sweet liquid of his own manufacture. On these occasions he appeared, not with his cork hat, but with a handkerchief knotted around his head. He rang a bell and sang his sales rhymes, which were often pure gibberish. 'Neighbour! Neighbour! Where are you? Here I am! Rat-tat-too.' Sometimes he would point to the poisonous tub in which hunks of ice floated in red liquid, and sing: 'Walk in! Jump in! Run in! Hop in! Flop in! Leap in! Creep in!'

This was the Mr Lambert of happier days. Now, after the degradation of his house, it seemed that he had given up his stall. But he had grown friendly with Mano and this friendship led him to announce that he was going to the sports meeting in which Mano was to take part.

Henry said, 'Mrs Lambert doesn't like it. She feel that this old black man hopping around with a handkerchief on his head and ringing his bell is a sort of low-rating, especially now that she building this new house. And she say that if he go and ring that bell any more she finish with him. She not going to let him set foot in the new house.'

So we were concerned about both Mr Lambert and Mano. We often went in the afternoons to the great park to cycle around with Mano as he walked, to help him to fight the impatience that made him run in walking races and get disqualified.

Henry said, 'Frankie, I think you trying too hard with Mano. You should watch it. You see what happen to Mrs Lambert. You know, I don't think people want to do what they say they want to do. I think we always make a lot of trouble for people by helping them to get what they say they want to get. Some people look at black people and only see black. You look at poor people and you only see poor. You think the only thing they want is money. All-you wrong, you know.'

One day while we were coming back in procession from the park, Mano pumping away beside us past the crocodile of Ma-Fo's children, we were horrified to see Mr Lambert stretched out on the pavement like a dead man. He was not dead; that was a relief. He was simply drunk, very complicatedly drunk. Selma ran to Mrs Lambert and brought back a cool message: 'Mrs Lambert says we are not to worry our heads with that good-for-nothing idler.'

Henry said, 'We are not doing Lambert any good by being so friendly with him. Mrs Lambert, I would say, is hostile to us all, definitely hostile.'

Mr Lambert at this stage revived a little and said, 'They say I am black. But black I am not. I tell you, good sirs, I am a Scot.'

Henry said, 'Is not so funny, you know. His grandfather was a big landowner, a big man. We even hear a rumour some years before the war that according to some funny law of succession Mr Lambert was the legal head of some Scottish clan.'

The house went up. The day of the sports meeting came. Mano was extremely nervous. As the time drew nearer he even began to look frightened. This was puzzling, because I had always thought him quite withdrawn, indifferent to success, failure or encouragement.

Henry said, 'You know, Mano never read the papers. On the road yesterday some crazy thing make him take up the evening paper and he look at the horoscope and he read: "You will be exalted today." '

'But that's nice,' I said.

'It get him frightened. Was a damn funny word for the paper to use. It make Mano think of God and the old keys of the kingdom.'

Mano was very frightened when we started for the sports ground. There was no sign in the street of Mr Lambert and we felt that he had in the end been scared off by Mrs Lambert and that to save face he had gone away for a little. But at the sports ground, after the meeting had begun and Mano was started on his walk – it was a long walk, and you must picture it going on and on, with lots of other sporting activities taking place at the same time, each activity unrelated to any other, creating a total effect of a futile multifarious frenzy – it was when Mano was well on his walk that we heard the bell begin to ring. To us it rang like doom.

'Mano will not run today, Mano will walk to heaven today.'

Exaltation was not in Mr Lambert's face alone or in his bell or in his words. It was also in his dress.

'On me some alien blood has spilt. I make a final statement, I wear a kilt.' And then came all his old rhymes.

And Mano didn't run. He walked and won. And Mr Lambert rang his bell and chanted: 'Mano will not run today. He will walk into the arms of his Lord today.'

We had worked for Mano's victory. Now that it had come it seemed unnatural. He himself was like a stunned man. He rejected congratulations. We offered him none. When we looked for Mr Lambert we couldn't find him. And with a sense of a double and deep unsettling of what was fixed and right, we walked home. We had a party. It turned into more than a party. We did not notice when Mano left us.

Later that night we found Mr Lambert drunk and sprawling on the pavement.

He said, 'I led her up from the gutter. I gave her bread, I gave her butter. And this is how she pays me back. White is white and black is black.'

We took him to his house. Henry went to see Mrs Lambert. It was no use. She refused to take him in. She refused to come out to him.

'To my own house I have no entrance. Come, friends, all on my grave dance.'

We had a double funeral the next day. Mano had done what so many others on the island had done. He had gone out swimming, far into the blue waters, beyond the possibility of return.

'You know,' Henry said, as we walked to the cemetery. 'The trouble with Mano was that he never had courage. He didn't want to be a walker. He really wanted to be a runner. But he didn't have the courage. So when he won the walking race, he went and drowned himself.'

Albert the postman was in our funeral procession. He said, 'News, Frankie. They send back another one of Blackwhite's books.'

Blackwhite heard. He said to me, 'Was your fault. You made me start writing about all *this*. Oh, I feel degraded. Who wants to read about this place?'

I said, 'Once you were all white, and that wasn't true. Now you are trying to be all black and that isn't true either. You are really a shade of grey, Blackwhite.'

'Hooray for me, to use one of your expressions. This place is nowhere. It is a place where everyone comes to die. But I am not like Mano. You are not going to kill me.'

'Blackwhite, you old virgin, I love you.'

'Virgin? How do you know?'

'We are birds of a feather.'

'Frankie, why do you drink? It's only a craving for sugar.'

'And I said to him: Dickie-bird, why do you weep? Sugar, sugar. A lovely word, sugar. I love its sweetness on my breath. I love its sweetness seeping through my skin.'

And in the funeral procession, which dislocated traffic and drew doffed hats and grave faces from passers-by, I wept for Mano and Lambert and myself, wept for my love of sugar; and Blackwhite wept for the same things and for his virginity. We walked side by side.

Selma said Henry was right. 'I don't think you should go around interfering any more in other people's lives. People don't really want what you think they want.'

'Right,' I said. 'From now on we will just live quietly.'

Quietly. It was a word with so many meanings. The quietness of the morning after, for instance, the spectacles on my nose, quiet in an abstemious corner. I was a character now. I had licence. Sugar sweetened me. In Henry's yard, in Selma's house, and on the sands of the desolate bay over the hills, the healing bay where the people of the island sought privacy for joy and grief.

Priest's denunciations of us, of me, grew fiercer. And Blackwhite, seen through the flapping curtain of his front room, pounded away at his typewriter in sympathetic rage.

Then one blurred aching morning I found on the front step a small coffin, and in the coffin a mutilated sailor doll and a toy wreath of rice fern.

They came around to look.

'Primitive,' Blackwhite said. 'Disgusting. A disgrace to us.'

'This is Priest work,' Henry said.

'I have been telling you to insure me,' Selma said.

'What, is that his game?'

Henry said, 'Priest does take his work seriously. The only thing is, I wish I know what his work is. I don't know whether it is preaching, or whether it is selling insurance. I don't think he know either. For him the two seem to come together.'

To tell the truth, the coffins on Selma's doorstep worried me. They kept on appearing and I didn't know what to do. Selma became more and more nervous. At one moment she suggested I should take her away; at another moment she said that I myself should go away. She also suggested that I should try to appease Priest by buying some insurance.

'Appease Priest? The words don't sound right. Henry, you hear?'

Henry said, 'I will tell you about this insurance. I don't know how it happen on the island, but it becoming a social thing, you know. Like having a shower, like taking schooling, like getting married. If you not insured these days you can't hold up your head at all. Everybody feel you poor as a church rat. But look. The man coming himself.'

It was Priest, wearing a suit and looking very gay and not at all malevolent.

'Dropping in for a little celebration,' he said.

Selma was awed, and it was hard to say whether it was because of Priest's suit, the coffins, or his grand manner.

'What are you celebrating?' I said. 'A funeral?'

He wasn't put out. 'New job, Frankie, new job. More money, you know. Higher commission, bigger salary. Frankie, where you say you living in the States? Well, look out for me. I might be going up there any day. So the bosses say.'

I said, 'I'd love to have you.'

'You know,' he said, 'how in this insurance business I have this marvellous record. But these local people' – and here he threw up his beard, scratched under his chin, screwed up his eyes – 'but these local people, you know how mean they is with the money. Then this new company come down, you know, and they get to know about me. I didn't go to see them. They send for me. And when I went to see them they treat me as a God, you know. And a damn lot of them was white to boot. You know, man, I was like – what I can say? – I was like a *playboy* in that crowd, a playboy. And look how the luck still with me, look how the luck still in my hand. You know what I come in here to celebrate especially? You know how for years I begging Ma-Ho to take out insurance. And you know how he, Ma-Ho, don't want to take out no insurance. He just saying he want to go back to China, back to the old wan-ton soup and Chiang Kai-shek. Well, he insured as from today.'

Henry said, 'He pass his medical?'

I said, 'Offhand, that man looks damn sick to me, you know.'

'He pass his medical,' Priest said.

'He went to the doctor?' Henry asked. 'Or the doctor went to him?'

'What you worrying with these de*tails*? You know these Chinese people. Put them in their little shop and they stay there until kingdom come. Is a healthy life, you know.'

Henry said. 'Ma-Ho tell me one day that when he come

to the island in 1920 and the ship stop in the bay and he look out and he see only mangrove, he started to cry.'

Selma said, 'I can't imagine Ma-Ho crying.'

Henry said, 'To me it look as though he never stop crying.'

'Offhand,' I said, 'no more coffins, eh?'

'Let me not hear of death,' Priest said in his preaching manner. He burst out laughing and slapped me on the back.

And, indeed, no more coffins and dead sailors and toy wreaths appeared on Selma's steps.

I knocked on Selma's door one day two weeks later. 'Any coffins today, Ma'am?'

'Not today, thank you.'

Selma had become houseproud. The little house glittered and smelt of all sorts of polishes. There were pictures in passe-partout frames on the walls and potted ferns in brass vases on the marble-topped three-legged tables for which she had a passion. That day she had something new to show me: a marble-topped dresser with a clay basin and ewer.

'Do you like it?'

'It's lovely. But do you really need it?'

'I always wanted one. My aunt always had one. I don't want to use it. I just want to look at it.'

'Fine.' And after a while I said, 'What are you going to do?'

'What do you mean?'

'Well, the war's not going to go on for ever. I can't stay here for ever.'

'Well, it's as Blackwhite says. You are going to go back, we are going to stay here. Don't weep for me, and' – she waved around at all the little possessions in her room – 'and I won't weep for you. No. That's not right. Let's weep a little.'

'I feel,' I said, 'that you are falling for old Blackwhite. He's talked you round, Selma. Let me warn you. He's no good. He's a virgin. Such men are dangerous.'

'Not Blackwhite. To tell you the truth, he frightens me a little.'

'More than Priest?'

'I am not frightened of Priest at all,' she said. 'You know, I always feel Priest handles the language like a scholar and gentleman.'

I was at the window. 'I wonder what you will say now.'

Priest was running down the street in his suit and howling: 'All-you listen, all-you listen. Ma-Ho dead, Ma-Ho dead.'

And from houses came the answering chant. 'Who dead?'

'Ma-Ho dead.'

'The man was good. Good, Good.'

'Who?'

'Ma-Ho.'

'I don't mean he was not bad. I mean,' Priest said, subsiding into personal grief, 'I mean he was well. He was strong. He was healthy. And now, and now, he dead.'

'Who dead?'

'Ma-Ho. I not crying because I blot my book in my new job. I not crying because this is the first time I sell insurance to someone who dead on my hands. I not crying because those white people did much me up when I get this new job.'

'But, Priest, it look so.'

'It look so, but it wrong. O my brothers, do not misunderstand. I cry for the man.'

'What man?'

'Ma-Ho.'

'He did want to go back.'

'Where?'

'China.'

'China?'

'China.'

'Poor Ma-Ho.'

'You know he have those Chinese pictures in the backroom behind the shop.'

'And plenty children.'

'And you know how nice the man was.'

'The man was nice.'

'You go to Ma-Ho and ask for a cent red butter. And he give you a big lump.'

'And a chunk of lard with it.'

'And he was always ready to give a little trust.'

'A little trust.'

'Now he dead.'

'Dead.'

'He not going to give any lard again.'

'No lard.'

'He not going to China again.'

'Dead.'

Through the roused street Priest went, howling from man to man, from woman to woman. And that evening under the eaves of Ma-Ho's shop, before the closed doors, he delivered a tremendous funeral oration. And his six little girls sang hymns. Afterwards he came in, sad and sobered, to Henry's and began to drink beer.

Henry said, 'To tell you the truth, Priest, I was shocked when I hear you sell Ma-Ho insurance. Is a wonder you didn't know the man had diabetes. But with all these coffins all over the place, I didn't think it was any of my business. So I just keep my mouth shut. I ain't say nothing. I always say everybody know their own business.'

'Diabetes?' Priest said, almost dipping his beard into his beer. 'But the doctor pass him in everything.' He made circular gestures with his right hand. 'The doctor give him a test and everything was correct. Everything get test. The man was good, good, good, I tell you. He was small, but all of all-you used to see him lifting those heavy sugar bags and flour bags over the counter.'

Henry asked, 'You did test his pee?'

'It was good. It was damned good pee.' Priest wept a little. 'You know how those Chinese people neat. He went into the little back-room with all those children, and he bring out a little bottle – a little Canadian Healing Oil bottle.' Still weeping, he indicated with his thumb and finger the size of the bottle.

'Was not his pee,' Henry said. 'That was why he didn't want to *go* to the doctor. That was why he wanted the doctor to come to *him*.'

'O God!' Priest said. 'O God! The Chinese bitch. He make me lose my bonus. And you, Henry. You black like me and you didn't tell me nothing. You see,' he said to the room, 'why black people don't progress in this place. No corporation.'

'Some people corporate in one way,' Henry said. 'Some people corporate in another way.'

'Priest,' I said, 'I want you to insure Selma for me.'

'No,' Selma said nervously. 'I don't want Priest to insure me. I feel the man blight.'

'Do not mock the fallen,' Priest said. 'Do not mock the fallen. I will leave. I will move to another part of the city. I will fade away. But not for long.'

And he did move to another area of the city. He became a nervous man, frightened of selling insurance, instilling terror, moreover, into those to whom he tried to sell insurance: the story of Ma-Ho's sudden death got around pretty quickly.

Ma-Ho went, and with him there also went the Chinese emblems in his shop. No longer the neat crocodile left and entered the back door of the shop; and from being people who kept themselves to themselves, who gave the impression of being only temporary residents on the island, always packed for departure, Ma-Ho's family came out. The girls began to ride bicycles. The insurance money was good. The boys began to play cricket on the pavement. And Mrs Ma-Ho, who had never spoken a word of English, revealed that she could speak the language.

'I begin to feel,' Blackwhite said, 'that I am wrong. I begin to feel that the island is just about beginning to have an existence in its own right.'

Our own flag was also about to go down. The war ended. And, after all these years, it seemed to end so suddenly. When the news came there was a Carnival. No need to hide now. Bands sprang out of everywhere. A song was created out of nothing: *Mary Ann*. And the local men, who had for so long seen the island taken over by others, sang, but without malice, 'Spote, spote, Yankee sufferer,' warning everyone of the local and lean times to come.

The atmosphere at Henry's subtly changed. Gradually through the boom war years there had been improvements. But now, too, the people who came changed. Officers came from the base with their wives, to look at the dancing. So did some of the island's middle class. Men with tape recorders sometimes appeared in the audience. And in the midst of this growing esteem, Henry became more and more miserable. He was a character at last, mentioned in the newspapers. The looser girls faded away; and more *wabeens* appeared, so expensive as to be indistinguishable from women doomed to marriage. Henry reported one day that one of his drummers, a man called Snake, had been seized by somebody's wife, put into a jacket and tie, and sent off to the United States to study music.

Henry, now himself increasingly clean and increasingly better shaven, was despondent. Success had come to him, and it made him frightened. And Blackwhite, who had for years said that people like Snake were letting down the island, adding to the happy-go-lucky-native idea, Blackwhite was infuriated. He used to say, 'Snake is doing a difficult thing, beating out music on dustbins. That is like cutting down a tree with a penknife and asking for applause.' Now, talking of the kidnapping of Snake, he spoke of the corruption of the island's culture.

'But you should be happy,' I said. 'Because this proves that the island exists.'

'No sooner exists,' he said, 'than we start to be destroyed. You know, I have been doing a lot of thinking. You know, Frankie, I begin to feel that what is wrong with my books is not me, but the language I use. You know, in English, black is a damn bad word. You talk of a black deed. How then can I write in this language?'

'I have told you already. You are getting too black for me.'

'What we want is our own language. I intend to write in our own language. You know this patois we have. Not English, not French, but something we have made up. This is our own. You were right. Damn those lords and ladies. Damn Jane Austen. This is ours, this is what we have to work with. And Henry, I am sure, whatever his reasons, is with me in this.'

'Yes,' Henry said. 'We must defend our culture.' And sadly regarding his new customers, he added: 'We must go back to the old days.'

On the board outside Blackwhite's house there appeared this additional line: PATOIS TAUGHT HERE.

Selma began going to the Imperial Institute to take sewing lessons. The first lessons were in hemstitching, I believe, and she was not very good. A pillowcase on which she was working progressed very slowly and grew dirtier and dirtier, so that I doubted whether in the end any washing could make it clean again. She was happy in her house, though, and was unwilling to talk about what was uppermost in my own mind: the fact that we at the base had to leave soon.

We did talk about it late one night when perhaps I was in no position to talk about anything. I had gone out alone, as I had often done. We all have our causes for irritation, and mine lay in this: that Selma refused to exercise any rights of possession over me. I was free to come and go as I wished. This had been a bad night. I could not get the key into the door; I collapsed on the steps. She let me in in the end. She was concerned and sympathetic, but not as concerned as she might have been. And yet that tiny moment of rescue stayed with me: that moment of helplessness and self-disgust and total despair at the door, which soon, to my scratchings, had miraculously opened.

We began by talking, not about my condition, but about her sewing lessons. She said, 'I will be able to earn a little money with my sewing after these lessons.'

I said, 'I can't see you earning a penny with your sewing.'

She said, 'Every evening in the country my aunt would sit down by the oil lamp and embroider. She looked very happy when she did this, very contented. And I promised myself that when I grew up I too would sit down every evening and embroider. But really I wonder, Frank, who is afraid for who.'

Again the undistorted reflection. I said, 'Selma, I don't think you have ever been nicer than you were tonight when you let me in.'

'I did nothing.'

'You were very nice.' Emotion is foolish and dangerous; the sweetness of it carried me away. 'If anyone ever hurts you, I'll kill him.'

She looked at me with amusement.

'I really will, I'll kill him.'

She began to laugh.

'Don't laugh.'

'I am not really laughing. But for this, for what you've just said, let us make a bargain. You will leave soon. But after you leave, whenever we meet again, and whatever has happened, let us make a bargain that we will spend the first night together.'

We left it at that.

So now there gathered at Henry's, more for the company than for the pleasure, and to celebrate what was changing, the four of us whose interests seemed to coincide: Henry, Blackwhite, Selma and myself. What changes, changes. We were not together for long. Strangers were appearing every day now on the street, and one day there appeared two who split us up, it seemed, forever.

We were at Henry's one day when a finely-suited middle-aged man came up hesitantly to our table and introduced himself as Mr de Ruyter of the Council for Colonial Cultures. He and Blackwhite got on well from the start. Blackwhite spoke of the need to develop the new island language. He said he had already done much work on it. He had begun to

'You are in one of your moods,' Blackwhite said. 'I don't think you can see that we have moved with the times.'

'Oh, I am frightened of you.'

'Drunkard,' Blackwhite said.

'It's only sugar, remember?'

'I believe, Frank, speaking as a friend, that you want another island. Another bunch of happy-go-lucky natives.'

'So you went to Cambridge?'

'A tedious place.'

'Still, it shows.'

The band began to tune up. Blackwhite became restless, anxious to get back to his guests. 'Come, Frankie, why don't you go down to the kitchen with Henry and have a drink and talk over old times? You can see we have some very distinguished guests from various foundations tonight. Very important negotiations on hand, boy. And we mustn't give them a wrong idea of the place, must we? Don't waste your time. Take a tip. Start looking for another island.' He looked at me; he softened. 'Though I don't think there is any place for you now except home. Take him down, Henry. And Henry, look, when Pablo and those other idlers come, clean them up a little bit in the kitchen first before you send them up, eh?'

Men and women in fancy costumes which were like the waiters' costumes came out on to the stage and began doing a fancy folk dance. They symbolically picked cotton, symbolically cut cane, symbolically carried water. They squatted and swayed on the floor and moaned a dirge. From time to time a figure with a white mask over his face ran among them, cracking a whip; and they lifted their hands in pretty fear.

'You see how us niggers suffered,' Henry said, leading me to a door marked STAFF ONLY. 'Is all Blackwhite doing, you know. He say it was you who give him the idea. You make him stop writing all those books about lords and ladies in England. You ask him to write about black people. You know, Frankie, come to think of it, you did interfere a damn lot, you know. Is a wonder you didn't try to marry me off. Is a *wonder*? Is a pity. Remember what you did use to say about what you would do if you had a million dollars? What you would do for the island, for the street?'

'A million dollars.'

Footsteps behind me. I turned.

'Frankie.'

'Leonard.'

'Frankie, I am glad I found you. I was really worried about you. But goodness, isn't this a terrific place? Did you see that last dance?'

From where we were we could hear the cracking of whips, orchestrated wails, the stamp and scuttling of feet. Then it came: muted, measured applause.

'Leonard, you'd better get back,' I said. 'There are some people from various foundations upstairs who have seized Mr White. If you aren't careful you will lose him.'

'Oh, is that who they were? Thanks for telling me. I will run up straight away. I don't know how I will make myself known to him. People just don't believe me . . .'

'You will think of something. Henry, where is the telephone?'

'You still play this telephone game. One day the police are going to catch up with you.'

I dialled. The telephone rang. I waited. A booming male voice shouted, 'Frankie. Stay away.' So loud that even Henry could hear.

'Priest,' I said. 'Gary Priestland. How do you think he knew?'

Henry said, 'From the way you've been getting on, I don't imagine there is a single person in town who doesn't know. You know you broke up the British Council lecture on Shakespeare or something?'

'My God.' I remembered the room. Six people, a man in khaki trousers swinging jolly, friendly legs over a table.

'You thought it was a bar.'

'But, Henry, what's happened to the place? You mean

they've actually begun to give you culture now? Shakespeare
and all the rest of it?'

'They give we, we give them. A two-way process, as old
Blackwhite always saying. And they always saying how
much they have to learn from us. I don't know how the thing
catch on so sudden. You see the place is like a little New
York now. I imagine that's why they like it. Everybody
feel at home. Ice-cubes in the fridge, and at the same time
they getting the exotic old culture. The old Coconut Grove
even have a board of governors. I think, you know, the next
thing is they going to ask me to run for the City Council.
They already make me a MBE, you know.'

'MBE?'

'Member of the Order of the British Empire. Something
they give singers and people in culture. Frankie, you don't
even care about the MBE. Forget the telephone. Forget
Selma. Sometimes you want the world to end. You can't go
back and do things again. They begin just like that, they get
good. The only thing is you never know they good until they
finish. I wish the hurricane would come and blow away all
this. I feel the world need this sort of thing every now and
then. A clean break, a fresh start. But the damn world don't
end. And we don't dead at the right time.'

'What about Selma?'

'You really want to know?'

'Tell me.'

'I hear she buy a mixmaster the other day.'

'Now this is what I really call news.'

'I don't know what else to tell you. I went the other day
to the Hilton. Barbecue night. I see Selma there, picking and
choosing with the rest. Everybody moving with the times,
Frankie. Only you and me moving backwards.'

Mrs Henry came into the room. She didn't have to say
that she didn't like me. Henry cringed.

She said, 'I don't know, Henry. Leave you in charge in
front for five minutes, and the place start going to pieces.
I just had to sack the doorman. He didn't have no tie or

anything. And Mr White did ask you to take special care this evening.'

I fingered the doorman's tie. When Mrs Henry left Henry sprayed the door with an imaginary tommy gun. I was aware of the room. We were among flowers. Hundreds of plastic blooms.

'You looking,' Henry said. 'Is not my doing. I like a flowers, but I don't like a flowers so bad.'

The back door was pushed open again. Henry cringed, lowered his voice. But it wasn't Mrs Henry.

'I is Pablo,' an angry man said. 'What that fat woman mean, telling we to come round by the back?'

'That was no woman,' Henry said. 'That was my wife.'

Pablo was one of three angry men. Three men of the people: freshly washed hair, freshly oiled, freshly suited. They looked like triplets.

Pablo said, 'Mr White sent for us specially. He send for me. He send for he.' He pointed to one of his friends.

The friend said, 'I is Sandro.'

'He send for he.'

'I is Pedro.'

'Pablo, Sandro, Pedro,' Henry said, 'cool down.'

'Mr White won't like it,' Pablo said.

'Making guests and artisses come through the back,' said Sandro.

'When they get invite to a little supper,' said Pedro.

Henry sized them up. 'Guests and artisses. A lil supper. Well, all-you look all right, I suppose. Making, as they say, the best of a bad job. Go up. Mr White waiting for you.'

They left, mollified. Determination to deter further insult was in their walk. Henry, following them, seemed to sag.

I noticed an angry face behind the window. It was the sacked doorman. I could scarcely recognize him without his tie. He made threatening gestures; he seemed about to climb in. I straightened his tie around my collar and hurried after Henry into the main hall.

At the long table the little supper seemed about to begin.

Blackwhite rose to meet Pablo, Sandro and Pedro. The three expensively-suited men with Blackwhite rose to be introduced. Leonard and Sinclair were hanging around uncertainly.

Blackwhite eyed Leonard. Leonard flinched. He saw me and ran over.

'I don't have the courage,' he whispered.

'I'll introduce you.'

I led him to the table.

'I'll introduce you,' I said again. 'Blackwhite is an old friend.'

I pulled up two chairs from another table. I put one chair on Blackwhite's right. For Leonard. One chair on Blackwhite's left. For me. Astonishment on the faces of the foundation men; anxiety on Blackwhite's; a mixture of assessment and sympathy on the faces of Pablo, Sandro and Pedro, uncomfortable among the crystal and linen, the flowers and the candles.

A waiter passed around menus. I tried to take one. He pulled it back. He looked at Blackwhite, questioning. Blackwhite looked at me. He looked down at Leonard. Leonard gave a little smile and a little wave and looked down at the table at a space between settings. He drew forks from his right and knives from his left.

'Yes,' Blackwhite said. 'I suppose. Feed them.'

They hurried up with knives and forks and spoons.

Pablo and Sandro and Pedro were lip-reading the menus.

Pablo said, 'Steak Chatto Brian for me.'

'But, sir,' the waiter said. 'That's for two.'

Pablo said, 'You didn't hear me? Chatto Brian.'

'Chatto Brian,' Sandro said.

'Chatto Brian,' Pedro said.

'Oysters,' I said. 'Fifty. No, a hundred.'

'As a starter?'

'And ender.'

'Prawns for me,' Leonard said. 'You know. Boiled. And with the shells. I like peeling them.'

'He is a great admirer of yours, Blackwhite,' I said. 'His name is Leonard. He is a patron of the arts.'

'Yes, indeed,' Leonard said. 'Mr White, this is a great pleasure. I think *Hate* is wonderful. It is – it is – a most *endearing* work.'

'It was not meant to be an endearing work,' Blackwhite said.

'Goodness, I hope I haven't said the wrong thing.'

'You can't, Leonard,' I said. 'Leonard has got some money to give away.'

Blackwhite adjusted the nature of his gaze. Pablo, Sandro and Pedro looked up. The men from the foundations stared.

'Do you know him, Chippy?'

'Can't say I do. I'll ask Bippy.'

'I don't know him, Tippy.'

'Leonard,' Chippy said. 'I've never heard of that name in Foundationland.'

'This is possible,' Blackwhite said. 'But Leonard has the right idea.'

'Mr White,' Bippy said, affronted.

'We have never let you down,' said Tippy.

'You won't want to run out on us now, will you, Mr White?' Chippy asked.

'What about you, Mr White?' asked the waiter.

Blackwhite considered the menu. 'I think I'll start with the Avocado Lucullus.'

'Avocado Lucullus.' The waiter made an approving note.

'What do you mean by the right idea, Mr White?'

'Then I think I'll try a sole. What's the bonne femme like tonight? The right idea?'

The waiter brought his thumb and index finger together to make a circle.

'Well, let's say the sole bonne femme. With a little spinach. Gentlemen, I'll tell you straight. The artist in the post-colonial era is in a position of peculiar difficulty.'

'How would you like the spinach, Mr White?'

'En branches. And the way you or anyone else can help

him is with – money. There it is, gentlemen. The way you
can help Pablo here – '

'The wine list, Mr White.'

'Go on. We are listening.'

'The way to help Pablo – ah, sommelier. But let's ask our
hosts.'

'No, no. We leave that to you, Mr White.'

'Is with – money. Shall we break some rules? Pablo, would
you and your boys mind a hock? Or would you absolutely
insist on a burgundy to go with your Chateaubriand?'

'Anything you say, Mr White.'

'I think the hock. Tell me, do you have any of that nice
Rudesheimer left?'

'Indeed, Mr White. Chilled.'

'All right, gentlemen? A trifle sweet. But still.'

'Sure. Waiter, bring a couple of bottles of what Mr White
just said. How do we help Pablo?'

'Pablo? You give Pablo ten thousand dollars. And let him
get on with the job.'

'What does he do?' asked Bippy.

'That's a de*tail*,' Blackwhite said. 'So far as my present
argument goes.'

'I entirely agree,' Chippy said.

'Waiter,' Blackwhite called. 'I believe you have forgotten
our hosts.'

'Sorry, gentlemen. For you?'

'But if you are interested, Pablo and his boys are a painting
group. They work together at the same time on one canvas.'

'Steak tartare. Like the Italians. Or the Dutch.'

'Steak tartare. One man painting the face.'

'Steak tartare. The other painting the scenery. Steak
tartare. What am I saying? Just a salad.'

'Not quite,' Blackwhite said. 'This is more an experiment
in recovering the tribal subconscious.'

'Shall we say, en vinaigrette?'

'What do you mean?'

'You know about Jung and the racial memory.'

'With vinegar.'

'That's just about how I feel.'

'They have produced some very interesting results. A sort of artistic stream-of-consciousness relay. But in paint. A sort of continuous mutual interference.'

'This sounds very interesting, Mr White,' Bippy said.

'We don't want to offend Pablo,' Tippy said.

'Or Sandro or Pedro,' Chippy added.

'But we have to be sure, Mr White.'

'Foundationland has its own rules, Mr White.'

'Mr White, we have to write reports.'

'Mr White, help us.'

'Mr White, we have made this journey to see *you*.'

'I don't know, gentlemen. We can't just *brush* off Pablo and his boys just like that. An appropriate word, don't you think? Let us see how they feel.'

Bippy, Tippy and Chippy looked at Pablo, Sandro and Pedro.

'Ask them,' Blackwhite said. 'Go on, ask them.'

'What do you feel about this, Mr Pablo?' Bippy asked.

'If any money going, give it to Blackwhite,' Pablo said.

'Give it to Mr White,' Sandro said.

'Is what I say too,' said Pedro.

'You see, Mr White,' Chippy said. 'You must shoulder your responsibilities. We appreciate your desire to nurse struggling talent. But – '

'Exactly,' said Tippy.

Blackwhite didn't look disappointed.

The food came. Pablo and his friends began sawing. Blackwhite scooped avocado, poured wine.

Blackwhite said, 'I didn't want it to appear that I was pushing myself forward. I wanted you to meet Pablo and his boys because I thought you might want to encourage something new. I feel that you chaps have got quite enough out of me as it is.'

There was a little dismissing laughter. I swallowed oysters. Leonard peeled prawns.

'And also,' Blackwhite went on, 'because I felt that you might not be altogether happy with the experimental work I have on hand.'

'Experimental?' Tippy said.

'Oh, this sounds good,' Leonard said.

'Gentlemen, no artist should repeat himself. My inter-racial romances, though I say it myself, have met with a fair amount of esteem, indeed acclaim.'

'Indeed,' said Bippy, Tippy and Chippy.

'Gentlemen, before you say anything, listen. I have decided to abandon the problem.'

'This is good,' Leonard said. 'This is very good.'

'How do we abandon the problem?' Blackwhite said.

Pablo reached forward and lifted up a wine bottle. It was empty. He held it against the light and shook it. Chippy took the bottle from him and set it on the table. 'There is nothing more there,' he said.

'I have thought about this for a long time. I think I should move with the times.'

'Good old Blackwhite,' I said.

'I want,' Blackwhite said, 'to write a novel about a black man.'

'Oh, good,' Leonard said.

'A novel about a black man falling in love.'

'Capital,' said Bippy, Tippy and Chippy.

'With a black woman.'

'Mr White!'

'Mr White!'

'Mr White!'

'I thought you would be taken aback,' Blackwhite said. 'But I would regard such a novel as the statement of a final emancipation.'

'It's a terrific idea,' Leonard said.

'Tremendous problems, of course,' Blackwhite said.

'Mr White!' Bippy said.

'We have to write too,' said Chippy.

'Our reports,' said Tippy.

'Calm down, boys,' Bippy said. 'Mr White, you couldn't tell us how you are going to treat this story?'

'That's my difficulty,' Blackwhite said.

'*Your* difficulty,' Chippy said. 'What about ours?'

'Black boy meets black girl,' Tippy said.

'They fall in love,' said Bippy.

'And have some black children,' said Chippy.

'Mr White, that's not a story.'

'It's more like the old-fashioned coon show. The thing we've been fighting against.'

'You'll have the liberals down your throat.'

'You will get us the sack. Mr White, look at it from our point of view.'

'Calm down, boys. Let me talk to him. This is a strange case of regression, Mr White.'

'I'll say. You've regressed right back to Uncle Remus, right back to Brer Rabbit and Brer Fox.'

'Do us another *Hate* and we'll support you to the hilt.'

'Give us more of the struggler, Mr White.'

'Calm *down*, boys. Much depends on the treatment, of course. The treatment is everything in a work of art.'

'Of course,' Blackwhite said, scooping up the bonne femme sauce from the dish in the waiter's reverential hand.

'I don't know. You might just work something. You might have the black man rescued from a bad white woman.'

'Or the black woman rescued from a bad white man.'

'Or *some*thing.'

'We've got to be careful,' Blackwhite said. 'I have gone into this thing pretty thoroughly. I don't want to offend any ethnic group.'

'What do you mean, Mr White?'

'He is right,' Leonard said. 'Mr White, I think you are terrific.'

'Thank you, Leonard. And also, I was toying with the idea of having a bad black man as my hero. Just toying.'

'Mr White!'

'Mr White!'

'Mr White!'

'I am sorry. I have used a foolish word. One gets into such a way of talking. Reducing the irreducible to simple terms. I don't mean bad. I just mean ordinary.'

'Mr White!'

'Calm down, Tippy.'

'What do you mean, Mr White? Someone bad at ball games?'

'And tone deaf?'

'You just want a cripple,' Leonard said.

'The thought occurred to me too, Leonard,' Blackwhite said. 'They just want a cripple.'

'Who the hell said anything about a cripple?'

'Calm down, Bippy.'

'Kid,' Chippy said. 'Forgive me for talking to you like this. But you are committing suicide. You've built up a nice little reputation. Why go and throw it away now for the sake of a few crazy ideas?'

'Why don't you go home and write us another *Shadowed Livery*?'

'Do us another *Hate*.'

Leonard said, 'I intend to support you, Mr White.'

Blackwhite said, 'I am rather glad this has turned out as it has. I believe I understand you gentlemen and what you stand for. It mightn't be a bad idea, after all, for you to extend your patronage to Pablo and his boys.'

'Anything to follow, Mr White?' the waiter said. 'A zabaglione? Crème de marrons?'

'I require nothing but the bill,' Blackwhite said. 'Though those boys look as though they require feeding.' He nodded towards Pablo and his friends.

The waiter produced the bill. Blackwhite waved towards Bippy, Tippy and Chippy, each of whom extended a trained hand to receive it.

'Mr White, we didn't mean to offend you.'

'But you have,' Leonard said.

'I hate you,' Blackwhite said to Bippy. He pointed to

Chippy. 'I hate you.' He pointed to Tippy. 'And I hate you.'
They began to smile.
'This is the old H. J. B. White.'
'We might have lost a friend.'
'But we feel we have saved an artist.'
'Feed Pablo and his boys from now on,' Blackwhite said.
'Yes,' Leonard said, rising. 'Feed Pablo. Mr White, I am
with you. I think your black idea is terrific. I will support
you. You will want for nothing.'
'Who is this guy?' Bippy asked.
'Thanks for the oysters,' I said. 'He's got a million to play
with. He's going to make you look pretty silly.'
'Who knows?' Chippy said. 'The mad idea might come
off.'
'New York won't like it if it does,' Bippy said.
'Calm down,' said Tippy.
They walked towards the bar.
'No more winter trips.'
'Or extended journeys.'
'No more congresses.'
'By day or night.'
'No more chewing over literate-chewer.'
'Or seminars on cinema.'
'But wait,' said Bippy. 'Perhaps Blackwhite was right.
Perhaps Pablo and his boys do have something. The tribal
subconscious.'
They were still eating.
'Mr Pablo?'
'Mr Sandro?'
'Mr Pedro?'

I left Blackwhite and Leonard together. I left Sinclair too.
He had been in the diningroom throughout. I went down to
the kitchen.
On the TV screen Gary Priestland was announcing: 'Here
is some important news. Hurricane Irene has altered course
fractionally. This means the island now lies in her path.

Irene, as you know' – he spoke almost affectionately – 'has flattened the islands of Cariba and Morocoy.' On the screen there appeared stills. Flattened houses; bodies; motor-cars in unlikely places; a coconut grove in which uprooted coconut trees lay almost parallel to one another as though laid there by design, to await erection. Gary Priestland gave details of death and injuries and financial loss. He was like a sports commentator, excited by a rising score. 'To keep you in touch the Island Television Service will not be closing down tonight. ITS will remain on the air, to keep you in constant touch with developments. I have a message from the Red Cross. But first – '

The Ma-Ho girls came on in their frilly short skirts and sang a brisk little whinnying song for a local rum.

While they were singing the telephone rang.

Henry had been gazing at the television set, held, it seemed, by more than news. He roused himself and answered the telephone.

'For you.'

'Frankie.'

The voice was not that of Gary Priestland, TV compere, master of ceremonies. It was the voice of Priest.

'Frankie, I am telling you. Stay away. Do not interfere. My thoughts are of nothing but death tonight. Leave Selma alone. Do not provoke her.'

On the TV I saw him put the telephone down, saw the manner change instantly from that of Priest to that of Priestland. Like a deity, then, he supervised more stills of disaster on the islands of Cariba and Morocoy.

The kitchen had a low ceiling. The light was fluorescent. No wind, no noise save that from the air extractor. The world was outside. Protection was inside.

Henry, gazing at the pictures of death and disorder, was becoming animated.

'Hurricane, Frankie. Hurricane, boy. Do you think it will really come?'

'Do you want it to come?'

He looked dazed.

I left him and made for the lavatories. The oyster sickness. One door carried a metal engraving of a man, the other of a woman. Their coyness irritated me. One at a time, they raced unsteadily up to me. I cuffed the woman. Squeals. I hurried through the door with the man.

The mirror was steamed over. I cleared part of it with my hand. For the first time that day, that night, that morning, I saw my face. My face, my eyes. My shirt, the doorman's tie. I was overwhelmed. The tribal subconscious. Portrait of the artist. I signed it in one corner.

'Yes. When all is said and done, I think you are pretty tremendous. Very brave. Moving among men like a man. You take taxis. You buy shirts. You run houses. You travel. You hear other people's voices and are not afraid. You are pretty terrific. Where do you get the courage?'

A hand on my elbow.

'Leonard,' I whispered, turning.

But it was Henry, a little firmer than he had been so far that evening, a little more rallying, a little less dejected.

'Hurricane coming, man. The first time. And you want to meet it here?'

I went out. And saw Selma.

'You,' I said.

'The mystery man on the telephone,' she said. 'No mystery to me, though, after the first few times. I knew it was you. Henry sent a message to me. I left the Hilton as soon as I could.'

'Barbecue night. Gary Priestland, master of ceremonies. I know. Selma, I have to talk to you. Selma, you have pulled down our house. I went and looked. You pulled it down.'

'I've got a nicer one.'

'Poor Selma.'

'Rich Selma,' Henry said. 'Poor Henry.'

We were in the kitchen. The television was blue. The air extractor roared.

'I sold the house to a foundation. They are going to put

up a national island theatre.' She nodded towards the television set. 'It was Gary's idea. It was a good deal.'

'You've all done good deals. Who is going to write the
plays? Gary?'

'It's only for happenings. No scenery or anything.
Audiences walking across the stage whenever they want.
Taking part even. Like Henry's in the old days.'

'Hurricane coming,' Henry said.

'It was all Gary's idea.'

'Not the hurricane,' I said.

'Even that.' She gazed at the screen as if to say, look.

Priestland, Priest, was lifting back his head. From details
of death and destruction on other islands, details delivered
with the messenger's thrill, he was rising to a type of religious exaltation. And now there followed not the Ma-Ho
girls with their commercials but six little black girls with
hymns.

She looked away. 'Come, shall I take you home?'

'You want me to see your home?'

'It is up to you.'

'Hurricane coming,' Henry said. He began to sway. 'All
this is over. We all become new men.'

'Repent!' Priest cried from the television screen.

'Repent?' Henry shouted back. 'All this is over.'

'Rejoice!' Priest said. 'All this is over.'

'Why run away now?' Henry said.

'Why run away?' Priest said. 'There is nothing to run to.
Soon there will be nothing to run from. There is a way which
seemeth right unto a man but at the end thereof are the ways
of death. Repent! Rejoice! How shall we escape, if we neglect
so great a salvation.'

'Emelda!' Henry called. 'Emelda!' To Selma and to me he
said, 'Not yet. Don't go. A last drink. A last drink. Emelda!'
He wandered about the kitchen and the adjoining room. 'All
these plastic flowers! All these furnitures! All these decorations! Consume them, O Lord!'

Mrs Henry appeared in the doorway.

'Emelda, my dear,' Henry said.

'What get into you now?'

He unhooked a flying bird from the wall and aimed it at her head. She ducked. The bird broke against the door.

'That cost forty dollars,' she said.

He aimed another at her. 'Eighty now.'

'Henry, the wind get in your head!'

'Let us make it a hundred.' He lifted a vase.

Selma said, 'Let us go.'

I said, 'I think the time has come.'

'No. You're my friends. You must have a farewell drink. Emelda, will you serve my friends?'

'Yes, Henry.'

'Call me mister, Emelda. Let us maintain the old ways.'

'Yes, Mr Henry.'

'Vodka and coconut water, Emelda.' He put down the vase. The black girls sang hymns.

'You let me in that night, Selma,' I said. 'I've remembered that.'

'I remember. That was why I came.'

Emelda, Mrs Henry, brought back a bottle, a pitcher and some tumblers.

Henry said, 'Emelda, after all this time you spend teaching me manners, you mean to want to give my friends glasses with hairs in it?'

'Then look after them yourself, you drunken old tout.'

'Old trout, old tout,' Henry said. And then, with shouts of pure joy, the hymns pouring out in the background, he smashed bottle, pitcher and tumblers. He went around breaking things. Emelda followed him, saying, 'That cost twenty dollars. That cost thirty-two dollars. That cost fifteen dollars. In a sale.'

'Sit down, Emelda.'

She sat down.

'Show them your mouth.'

She opened her mouth.

'Nice and wide. Is a big mouth you have, you know,

Emelda. The dentist could just climb in inside with his lunch parcel and scrape away all day.'

Emelda had no teeth.

'Frankie, look at what you leave me with. Sit down, Emelda. She and she sister setting competition. Sister take out all her teeth. So naturally Miss Emelda don't want to keep a single one of she own. Look. I got to watch this morning, noon and night. I mad to hit you, mouth. Mouth, I mad to hit you.'

'No, Henry. That mouth cost almost a thousand dollars, you know.'

'All that, and the world ending!'

'Rejoice!' Priest called from the television screen. He lifted the telephone on his desk and dialled.

The telephone in Henry's kitchen rang.

'Don't answer,' Selma said. 'Come, our bargain. Our first evening. Let me take you home.'

Hymns from the blue screen; screams from Emelda; the crash of glasses and crockery. The main room of The Coconut Grove, all its lights still on, was deserted. The thatched stage was empty.

'The perfection of drama. No scenery. No play. No audience. Let us watch.'

She led me outside. People here. Some from the Coconut Grove, some from neighbouring buildings. They stood still and silent.

'Like an aquarium,' Selma said.

Low, dark clouds raced. The light ever changed.

'Your car, Selma?'

'I always wanted a sports model.'

'The car is the man, is the woman. Where are you taking me to?'

'Home.'

'You haven't told me. Where is that?'

'Manhattan Park. A new area. It used to be a citrus plantation. The lots are big, half an acre.'

'Lovely lawns and gardens?'

'People are going in a lot for shrubs these days. It's something you must have noticed. You'll like the area. It's very nice.'

It was a nice area, and Selma's house was in the modernistic style of the island. Lawn, garden, a swimming pool shaped like a tear-drop. The roof of the veranda was supported on sloping lengths of tubular metal. The ceiling was in varnished pitchpine. The furnishings were equally contemporary. Little bits of driftwood; electric lights pretending to be oil lamps; irregularly shaped tables whose tops were sections of tree trunks complete with bark. She certainly hated straight lines and circles and rectangles and ovals.

'Where do you get the courage, Selma?'

'This is just your mood. We all have the courage.'

Local paintings on the wall, contemporary like anything.

'I always think women have a lot of courage. Imagine putting on the latest outrageous thing and walking out in that. That takes courage.'

'But you have managed. What do you sell? I am sure that you sell things.'

'Encyclopaedias. Textbooks. Inoffensive culture. *Huckleberry Finn* without nigger Jim, for ten cents.'

'You see. That's something I could never do. The world isn't a frightening place, really. People are playing a lot of the time. Once you realize that, you begin to see that people are just like yourself. Not stronger or weaker.'

'Oh, they are stronger than me. Blackwhite, Priest, you, even Henry – you are all stronger than me.'

'You are looking at the driftwood? Lovely things can be found in Nature.'

'But we don't leave it there. Lovely house, Selma. Lovely, ghastly, sickening, terrible home.'

'My home is not terrible.'

'No, of course not to you.'

'You can't insult me. You are too damn frightened. You don't like homes. You prefer houses. To fit into other people's lives.'

'Yes. I prefer houses. My God. I am on a treadmill. I can't get off. I am surrounded by other people's very big names.'

'You are getting worse, Frank. Come. Be a good boy. Bargain, remember. Let me show you my bedroom.'

'Adultery has its own rules. Never on the matrimonial bed.'

'Not matrimonial yet. That is to come.'

'I have no exalted idea of my prowess.'

'You were always lousy as a lover. But still.'

'What language, Selma. So snappy, man. Let me put on the old TV. I don't want to miss anything.'

The man on the screen had changed his clothes. He was wearing a white gown. He had abandoned news; he was only preaching.

He said, 'All we like sheep have gone astray; we have turned everyone to his own way.'

As if in sympathy with his undress, I began unbuttoning my shirt.

In the bedroom it was possible to hear him squawking on. On the bed lay a quilted satin eiderdown.

'You are like Norma Shearer in *Escape*.'

'Shut up. Come. Be good.'

'I will be good if I come.'

Our love-making was not a success.

'I was bad.'

'Drink is good for a woman,' Selma said. 'Bad for a man. You prepared yourself too well today, Frank. You waste your courage in fear.'

'I waste my courage in fear. "Now *look* what you have done."'

'Explain.'

'It was what a woman said to me many years ago. I was fifteen. She called me in one afternoon when I was coming back from school and asked me to get on top of her. And that was what she said at the end. "Now *look* what you have done." As though *I* had done the asking. Talking to me as though she was talking to a baby. Terrible. Sex is a hideous thing. I've decided. I'm anti-sex.'

'That makes two of us.'

'All I can say is that we've been behaving strangely for a very long time.'

'You started it. Tell me, did you expect me to keep our bargain?'

'I don't know. It is like one of those stories you hear. That a woman always sleeps with the man who took her maidenhead. Is it true? I don't know. Is it true?'

'It is,' Selma said, rising from the bed, 'an old wives' tale.'

In the drawingroom the television still groaned on. The black girls sang hymns. I went to the bathroom. The mat said RESERVED FOR DRIPS. On the lavatory seat there was a notice, flowers painted among the words: GENTLEMEN LIFT THE SEAT IT IS SHORTER THAN YOU THINK LADIES REMAIN SEATED THROUGHOUT THE PERFORMANCE. An ashtray; a little book of lavatory and bedroom jokes. The two so often going together. Poor Selma. I pulled the lavatory chain twice.

The wind was high.

'Selma, be weak like me. Henry is right. Priest is right. It is all going to be laid flat. Let us rejoice. Let us go to the bay. Let us take Henry with us. And afterwards, if there is an afterwards, Henry will take us to his pretty little island.'

'There are no more islands. It's not you talking. It's the wind.'

The oil lamp which was really an electric lamp was overturned. Darkness, except for the blue of the television screen. And the wind drowned Priest's voice.

Selma became hysterical.

'Let us get out of here. Let us go back to town. In the street with the others.'

'No, let us go to the bay.'

Henry sat among disarrayed plastic flowers, in a deserted Coconut Grove.

'The bay!'

'The bay.'

We drove up and over the hills, the three of us. We heard the wind. We ran down on to the beach, and heard the sea. At least that couldn't be changed. Once the beach was dangerous with coconut trees, dropping nuts. Now most had been cut down to make a parking lot. Standing foursquare on the beach was a great concrete pavilion, derelict: a bit of modernity that had failed: a tourist convenience that had served no purpose. The village had grown. It had spread down almost to the beach, a rural marine slum. Lights were on in many of the shacks.

'I never thought you could destroy the bay.'

'We might have a chance to start afresh.'

We walked in the wind. Pariah dogs came up to wait, to follow fearfully. The smell of rotting fish came fitfully with the wind. We decided to spend the night in the tourist pavilion.

Morning, dark and turbulent, revealed the full dereliction of the beach. Fishing boats reclined or were propped up on the sand that was still golden, but there were also yellow oil drums on the beach for the refuse of the fishermen, whose houses, of unplastered hollow-clay bricks and unpainted timber, jostled right up to the limit of dry sand. The sand was scuffed and marked and bloody like an arena; it was littered with the heads and entrails of fish. Mangy pariah dogs, all rib and bone, all bleached to a nondescript fawn colour, moved listlessly, their tails between their legs, from drum to yellow drum. Black vultures weighed down the branches of coconut trees; some hopped awkwardly on the sand; many more circled overhead.

Henry was peeing into the sea.

I called out to him, 'Let us go back. It is more than I can stand.'

'I always wanted to do this,' he said. 'In public.'

'You mustn't blame yourself,' Selma said. 'It is never very good in the morning.'

It hadn't been good.

We drove back to the city. We drove, always, under a low

dark sky. It was early, yet the island was alive. The streets were full of people. Their first hurricane, their first drama, and they had come out into the streets so as to miss nothing. All normal activity had been suspended. It was like a continuation of the night before; the streets were even more like aquaria, thick with life, but silent. Only the absence of the blackness of night seemed to have marked the passage of time; only that and the screens, now blank, of television sets seen through the open doors of houses – some still with useless lights on – and in cafés doing no business.

Then it was night again. The useless lights had meaning. Against the black sky blacker points moved endlessly: all the birds of the island, flying south. It was like the final abandonment. We were in the midst of noise, in which it was at times possible to distinguish the individual groans of houses, trees, and the metallic flapping of loose corrugated-iron sheets. No fear on any face, though. Only wonder and expectation.

The television screens shimmered. Priest reappeared, tired, shining with fatigue, telling us what we already knew, that the end of our world was at hand.

'Behold,' he said, 'now is the day of salvation.'

The city responded. Faintly at first, like distant temple bells, the sound of steel orchestras came above the roar of the wind. The pariah dogs, and those dogs that lived in houses, began to bark in relay, back and forth and crossways. Feet began to shuffle. Priest railed like a seer, exhausted by the effort of concentration. He railed; the city was convulsed with music and dance.

The world was ending and the cries that greeted this end were cries of joy. We all began to dance. We saw dances such as we had seen in the old days in Henry's yard. No picking of cotton, no cutting of cane; no carrying of water, no orchestrated wails. We danced with earnestness. We did contortions of which we had never thought ourselves capable.

We saw Blackwhite dancing with Leonard. Blackwhite not white, not black, but Blackwhite as we all would have liked to see him, a man released from endeavour, released from the strain of seeing himself (portrait of the artist: the tribal subconscious), at peace with the world, accepting, like Leonard. We saw Bippy, Tippy and Chippy arm in arm with Pablo, Sandro and Pedro, as though the wooing that had begun at The Coconut Grove had gone on all night: a gesture now without meaning, a fixed attitude of ritual in which news of the hurricane had caught them all. Occasionally the men from Foundationland pleaded with Blackwhite. Still, without malice or triumph, he spurned them, and did stylized stamps of simple negation: a private man, at last. As on a flat stage, stretching to infinity before our eyes, infinity the point where the painted floorboards met, companionship and wooing and pursuit and evasion played back and forth before us. But Leonard, obstinately dancing, dancing with earnestness, like the man anxious to catch the right mood and do the right thing: Leonard remained, in spite of his exertions, what he had always been, bemused, kind, blank. Arm in arm he danced with Blackwhite whenever they met; and Sinclair, big, heavy Sinclair, swung between them. And the tourist teams of the day before: the happy now like people who had forgotten the meaning of the word, which implied an opposite, the embittered, oh, infinitely less so. And for me, no terror of sky and trees: the courage of futility, the futility of courage, the empty, total response.

Through the streets, flattened to stage-boards, we danced, waiting for the final benediction. The sky hung low, grew high, hung low. The wind sweetly filled our ears, slackened, filled our ears again. We danced and waited. We waited and danced.

Benediction never came. Our dancing grew listless. Fatigue consumed anguish. But hope was not entirely consumed, even when on the television sets we saw Priest being transformed into Priestland, the seer into the newscaster, the man whose thoughts had only been of death, into the man who diminished life. But how could we deny?

We gave up the hurricane. We sat in the streets. Light

was grey, then silver. The stage was becoming a street again; houses took on volume. I heard Bippy, Tippy and Chippy wailing. Pablo and the boys comforted them.

Sinclair straightened his jacket and tie. In the light of a day that had now truly broken he went to Leonard, detached him from Blackwhite, and said, 'Come, Leonard. Come, boy. We have had our fun. It is time to go home!'

'Goodbye, Mr White,' Leonard said. 'Very well, Sinclair. You have been very good. Let us go.'

Blackwhite saw and understood. 'Leonard!' he said, stupefied. 'Leonard, what about my black novel? You promised help. You drove away the men from Foundation-land. You said I was to want for nothing.'

'Goodbye, Mr White. How are you feeling, Sinclair?'

'Leonard! You promised support! Bippy, Tippy, Chippy. Wait, wait. Pablo, call off your idlers! Pablo! Bippy! Mr Tippy! Mr Chippy!'

He, once the pursued, now became the pursuer. Pablo, Sandro and Pedro fled before him, as did Bippy, Tippy and Chippy. He pursued them; they evaded him and often the six came together. On the stage stretching to infinity the chase took place, pursuer and the six pursued dwindling to nothing before us. The sun was bright; there were shadows.

I went with Selma to The Coconut Grove. Henry was cleaning up the kitchen. Emelda stood over him. He re-arranged plastic flowers; he put broken vases together.

On the television set Gary Priestland was announcing that the hurricane had not come. But he had news for us, news of the destruction of some other island. He had news. He had facts and the figures of death. He had stills.

In the harbour the ships blew the all-clear.

The Ma-Ho girls came on and did a commercial for a local cigarette.

The programmes for the day were announced.

'Home,' Selma said.

'The old driftwood calls. Lovely things can be found in Nature.'

'Gary will be tired.'

'I'll say.'

And in the city where each exhausted person had once more to accommodate himself to his fate, to the life that had not been arrested, I went back to the hotel.

Hilton, Hilton.

Sailing 1 p.m., the board said in the lobby.

Moore-McCormack, Moore-McCormack.

August 1965